*Johnny Stevens Pioneer Adventures*

# A Spoonful of Dirt

## Joel Schnoor

**GP**
**Gennesaret Press**

Gennesaret Press
202 Persimmon Place
Apex, NC 27523

www.GennesaretPress.com

ISBN: 978-0-9845541-5-7

Library of Congress Control Number: 2014906224

Printed in the United States of America
Apex, North Carolina

Cover design by Nathan Schnoor
Illustrations by Derrick Eason

*To my wife Michelle*

# Table of Contents

# Preface

I grew up in a family of storytellers. My mother, especially, would weave family tales into the fabric of our conscious heritage so that the memories of those who went before us might not get lost in the passing of time. It is important to remember who our ancestors were and the struggles they faced in carving out a society in the rugged West. Overcoming a seemingly endless battery of challenges, they put their faith in God and met life one day at a time.

Mom particularly enjoyed telling tales of her grandfather, John Stevens, Jr., and over time she found various letters and stories that he wrote. The main character of this book, ten-year-old Johnny Stevens, is loosely based on the image of this man that has formed in my mind as a result of those stories.

Staunch adherents to the accuracy of the family heritage will wince at some of the liberties I have taken, but the essence of the stories remains true to the family heritage. The Stevens family was—and is—a no-nonsense clan of honest, hard-working folks who stuck together ("in all kinds of weather") and who relied on God for daily sustenance.

In a 1947 letter to his niece Lillian Blanche Stevens, John Stevens, Jr., wrote: "I am so glad you are taking some interest in ancestors, and I wish I had gotten the bug when the older folks were alive to help me. I can answer your questions as far as you have gone, and when I have time to look a little farther I will send you more facts. Uncle Ott was really our family historian, but he had such a lively imagination that I never knew where to draw the line between history and mythology."

Without further adieu, let me introduce my great-grandfather, John Stevens, Jr., to you. Here's Johnny.

Joel Schnoor
February 7, 2014

# 1

# Taking on the South

Early January, 1877

"Captain Johnny! Those Tar Heel boys have me sur-rounded and they're charging up the mountain!" Sam's voice rang out across the field, piercing the cool, early January air.

"Sam, I'm coming! Hold 'em off as long as you can! I'll save you!"

I turned to the right and yelled, "Captain Jones, take your men around the right flank. Captain Benson, you take the left flank." I looked straight ahead and, with steeled de-termination, I clenched my teeth and said, "And I'll take 'em right down the middle. Let's go, boys!"

With a whoop, I picked up the old, battered sled and started to run down the snowy slope. Running about as fast as my legs could carry me, I held the sled in front of me and dove onto it. The sled picked up speed quickly on the packed snow as I flew toward my foe, the perilous First North Carolina Cavalry. The rebels had Sam in a heap of trouble, but I knew that if I hit the snow bank just right I could wipe out the enemy forces, saving Sam and perhaps winning the war single-handedly.

The pile of snow exploded as I hit it at full speed. Those Rebel soldiers were scattered in every direction.

"You got 'em, Johnny Stevens!" Sam shouted. "Woo hoo!"

"Are you injured, Sam? How bad did they get you?" I asked, climbing out of the pile and brushing the snow off my head and shoulders.

"Took a bullet in the shoulder, another in the leg, one right here behind my ear, and one right in the stomach, but I think I can make it," Sam said with a grin.

Sam Hudson—my best friend in the world—and I spent as much time together as we could, fishing and playing down by the creek and the adjoining fields. The creek was a second home for both of us. Sam's family rented the farm with the white house on the north side of the creek, and we rented the farm with the red house on the south side of the creek. Sam and I spent many a hot summer night down at the creek, trying to hook a big catfish or taking a swim to cool off.

Summertime wouldn't come for months though. The cold January winters in Iowa felt about as far away from summer as a boy is from being an adult. In spite of the brutal temperatures, we reveled in playing outside in the snow.

Sam and I especially enjoyed pretending we were the Union army, going after the Confederate army with about as much gusto as two ten-year-olds could muster. We figured we knew something about battles, since our fathers had served in the same outfit—Company A of the First Iowa Infantry, out of Polk City, Iowa—in the Great Rebellion, which had ended nearly a dozen years earlier.

On that cold but sunny afternoon, Sam and I were taking turns riding the sled down the hill, crashing into a mountain of snow that we had built near the creek. Sam and I restored the snow pile, preparing it for the next battle.

"Hold on, sounds like more are coming over the ridge. It might be the Fourth Mississippi Cavalry. Sam, can you take 'em?"

Sam knelt down on the ground and put the side of his face in the snow, as though he were listening to something. "Johnny, that sounds like more than just the Fourth Mississippi Cavalry. If I'm not mistaken, it's the Fourth Mississippi, the Eleventh Tennessee Cavalry, and an Alabama regiment thrown in for good measure. They're marching with grit and determination."

"You mean grits and determination, don't you, Sam? This could be trouble. Better call in the reinforcements."

"You're right, Johnny. Good plan. Come on, Old Jack, let's go!"

Old Jack, my three-year-old yellow dog and companion, yelped as though he were agreeing with everything we said.

Sam picked up the sled, and the two of us ran back up the hill, led by Old Jack. At the top, I lay down on the sled. Sam gave me a push, and then he ran and dove on top of me. The two of us were speeding down the hill toward the pile of snow, with Old Jack right on our tail.

With two of us on the sled, we barreled through the snow pile and kept right on going toward the creek!

"Jump, Johnny!" Sam yelled, rolling off my right side.

I rolled off to the left side, sliding to a stop on the edge of the creek bank. The sled flew over the side of the creek, bounced on the ice, and hit the opposite bank with a thud.

"Good work, partner," exclaimed Sam. "They had us cornered and I thought we were goners, but it looks like we've decimated the Mississippi, Tennessee, and Alabama regiments."

Sam and I played and laughed until our sides ached as we rode that sturdy sled down the hill, over and over again. Finally, worn out, we sat down against the big double-trunked cottonwood that stood on the edge of the creek. Facing away from the wind and surveying the open field where we had just defeated a formidable foe, we let down our guard and basked in the glory of our battle. That turned out to be a tactical mistake.

"I figure we pretty much wiped out the southern forces, Captain Johnny."

"I suspect we did, Captain Sam. I reckon that we might have even won the whole war."

At that moment I heard footsteps, but I didn't turn around in time. Before we could move out of the way and defend ourselves, somebody dumped a large pail of powdery snow on us. I brushed the snow away from my eyes and looked at Sam; he shook his head, blinked his eyes, and looked at me.

"Kate!" we yelled in unison, jumping up to capture my little sister, but she had dropped the pail and had begun running back to the house, giggling with such a happy sound that both Sam and I just stood there laughing.

After Kate had put some distance between us, she turned and shouted, "'Bout time to eat, Johnny. Ma wants you to come help."

"Sounds like you have an important mission, Captain Johnny," said Sam, putting his hand on my shoulder.

"Yes sir, I do indeed. I reckon they need my advice on how to stop the advancing Georgia army."

"Either that, or they need you to fire up the stove and stir the beans."

"Whatever I need to do for the Union Army is my duty."

"And honor."

"And honor, yes sir."

"Good night, Johnny Stevens."

"Good night, Sam Hudson."

We saluted and then headed off in opposite directions. "Come on, Old Jack. Time to report back to camp."

Old Jack raced ahead. He could smell supper cooking.

The steam from my breath rose and then disappeared upward like little smoke signals sent to a big, big sky. Twinkling, the stars responded by faintly appearing, one by one, in the darkening twilight. I heard nothing but silence around me except for the soft crunch, crunch, crunch of the fresh powder beneath my feet as I walked along the creek, dragging my sled toward home.

I thought about the war and what it must have been like, charging into the enemy lines or hearing the whistle of a bullet that just missed. Pa had fought at Corinth and Vicksburg, and some of my friends would tell stories that their fathers had told them. Pa never talked about it much, though. I asked him about it once, and he said that sitting in a snow bank with no overcoat and no food and getting shot at by the enemy isn't as much fun as everyone makes it out to be. He also said that everybody has new battles to fight all the time and that he'd rather forget those battles of the past.

I hadn't seen any battles yet, and I sometimes wondered what they would be. I knew that every time Sam and I battled the South in our own version of the war, it seemed that the world became a little bit better.

Before I turned away from the creek and headed up the slope toward the house, I paused and looked around me. The accent of white snow outlined the boughs and branches of dark, barren trees; tracks in the snow proclaimed an abundance of animal life; and the soft orange glow of the pale winter sun melted into the horizon. No artist could have captured this scene; no imagination could have dreamed it. God had created that moment just for me. I couldn't imagine anything more perfect. Maybe it was too perfect. I found myself wishing it would last forever, and then suddenly I felt afraid that it wouldn't. Chilled from the increasing shadows along the creek, I turned and ran up the hill toward home.

# 2

# Family

"We won the war!" I said with a smile as I stepped into the house.

"You have kept us safe for another day, then," laughed Ma as she cooked supper on the stove. "Hang your coat by the fire to dry, Johnny."

"Yes ma'am."

I could hear the wind piercing the walls of our drafty house, and even with a fireplace full of hot coals, cold on the outside meant cold on the inside—and Iowa winter nights can get about as cold as they come.

Grandma Shideler, sitting next to the fireplace and wrapped up in a blanket, looked up at me and smiled.

"Johnny, let me warm your cheeks."

I gave her a hug and put my frozen cheeks against hers, rosy and warm from the fire.

"I like it when you warm my cheeks, Grandma."

"I think I like it even more than you do, Johnny. Did you have fun playing with Sam?"

"Yes ma'am, I sure did," I replied.

"Did you beat those Georgia boys?" she asked, with a look of mock concern on her face. "Or were you tangling with those rascals from Arkansas?"

"Didn't see them today, Grandma. We had to deal with some Carolina rebels and then a mess of combined Mississippi, Tennessee, and Alabama regiments."

"Sounds rough. Did you have many casualties?"

"No ma'am. We pretty much wiped them out without taking any losses ourselves."

"Whew. I'm glad you are protecting our household, Captain Johnny," she said with a laugh, her deep brown eyes twinkling in the fire light.

"Country, Grandma. I'm defending the whole country, not just the household," I said with a look of pride.

I liked being with Grandma. In her eighties, Grandma had lived with us ever since Grandpa had died, long before I could remember.

"Where are the others?" I asked, looking around. The house was uncharacteristically quiet.

"Kate's probably in the barn with the boys. I told her to fetch all of you in for supper and to make sure the animals are in for the night," said Ma. "Johnny, slice the bread please."

When I went to the stove to get the bread, I saw a platter filled with something brown and crumbly. "What's this, Ma?" I asked.

"What do you think it is?"

"Well, it looks kind of like dirt."

"Wouldn't that be something if your mother made dirt for dessert, Johnny?" Grandma cackled.

"It kind of does look like dirt, doesn't it?" Ma agreed. "Well, I tried a new chocolate spice cake recipe that didn't quite work out. The cake fell apart when I removed it from the pan."

The door flew open and in walked Elias and Ott, each carrying an armload of firewood. Kate was right behind.

"It's time to eat," announced Ma.

"Catherine, I think I'll just have my supper over here by the fireplace if you don't mind," said Grandma. "I'm feeling a bit chilled."

"Grandma, are you okay?" I asked.

"Oh, I think so, Johnny. I'm just worn out," she sighed, "and when I get worn out, I get cold. I'm anxious for spring to get here. These winters chill my old bones."

"Johnny, put the bread on the table," Ma said. "Kate, bring the pitcher of milk." Ma removed the lid from the pot on the stove, and it smelled awfully good.

"You may all sit down now," said Ma in her usual way. We children all sat down at the table, and Ma scooped stew into each of our bowls before sitting down at the end of the table closest to the stove. Pa usually sat at the opposite end near the door, but he and George—at seventeen, the oldest of us children—had taken the wagon to Des Moines to help a family move to Polk City.

"Elias, would you bless this meal?" asked Ma.

We closed our eyes and Elias, the next eldest at sixteen, began.

"Oh Heavenly Father, we thank you for the food we are about to receive. It is with humble hearts that we thank you for blessing us with the hunting skills necessary to provide this meal."

I looked up a moment at Elias. A seasoned hunter and a fine shot with the rifle, Elias did not mind letting everybody else know it. He had probably hunted the meat that we were about to eat. I closed my eyes and lowered my head as Elias continued.

"And we thank you for the bodies you have given us, healthy bodies capable of doing a goodly amount of work, and I pray that we would obey your desire that all of us work hard, whether it is chopping firewood, milking the cow, or repairing a broken trough in the barn."

Elias cleared his throat after listing the chores he had accomplished during the day. He had not yet mentioned sharpening the hatchet, which he had also done.

"Oh yes, and sharpening the hatchet," Elias added, as if on cue. Not hesitant to really put his shoulder into something that needed to be done—as long as it had nothing to do with schoolwork—Elias worked about as hard as anybody on the planet.

He continued. "Help us so that we are not prone to laziness—and Lord, especially be with Johnny and Kate, who still would rather play than work. And don't forget Ott, who would rather take a nap in the barn than do his chores."

At that moment, something struck me sharply in the shin.

"Ouch!" I shouted. "Who kicked me?"

"Not me," protested Ott.

"And not I," said Ma. "Kate, apologize to your brother."

"Sorry Johnny. I meant to get Elias," said Kate, in a very unapologetic tone of voice. "He's acting like a little rooster when the big rooster isn't around."

"Now children! We are saying grace. Please behave."

"Yes ma'am," both Kate and I replied.

"Elias, don't stray," reminded Ma, "and don't be prideful."

"Yes, Ma," said Elias, a bit smugly. He closed his eyes again. "And we pray for a safe return for Pa and George. In these and in everything, we give you thanks, Father. Amen."

The rest of us echoed the amen, and eating commenced. We had been silent at the table for almost a minute when Kate spoke up. "Ott, I know something that you don't know." Her light brown hair pulled back in braids made her blue eyes seem a little brighter.

Ott smiled. He always smiled, and sometimes I worried that his cheeks might wear out from all that smiling. At fifteen and the funny one of the bunch, Ott always had a joke ready that could get you to laughing until your side hurt. Nobody ever stayed mad at Ott for long.

Looking at Kate's eyes in a serious way, Ott responded, "I'll bet you do know something that I don't know, Kate. I think you know more than I do about a lot of things."

At nine years old and about as tough as they come, Kate could hold her own with pretty much anybody. Ott could baffle her, though, and he enjoyed toying with her in a good-humored way.

"Do you want to hear it?" asked Kate.

"It depends," replied Ott, "if it's something good or something bad."

"Well, I don't know if it's good or bad."

"Okay, then why don't you let me know what it is, and I'll tell you whether it's good or bad, and if it's good you can go ahead and tell me, but if it's bad then you don't have to say anything."

Kate sat there in silence, and then she screwed up her face in a quizzical way that set us all to laughing.

I heard Grandma softly chuckling over by the fireplace.

"Okay, I'll tell you," whispered Kate. "Ma, is it okay if I tell Ott something secret?"

"Secret?" asked Ma, amused. "Are you sure it's okay to tell someone's secret?"

"Well, it's not really someone's secret. It's Ott's secret, only Ott doesn't know it yet."

"Well, then I guess it's up to Ott, and if he says it's okay, then it's okay." Ma smiled, obviously enjoying this conversation.

Ott nodded. "Go ahead, Kate."

"Well Ott, Nellie Helms told me at school yesterday that Lizzie Zerr told her that Dora Summey's sister Madgie likes you."

Ott smiled, probably not surprised—all the girls at school and at church and everywhere else liked Ott. Ott had gotten used to being on the lookout so that he could hide if there were girls around. At his age, the girls paid a lot more attention to Ott than he did to them.

"Kate, that's very interesting. Well, I have a message that you can give to Nellie Helms."

Kate's eyes lit up. "What is it?"

"Tell Nellie Helms that your mother's husband's youngest son's youngest older brother says thank you for that piece of information."

Now Kate looked confused, and we all laughed. She asked him to repeat it, which he did five times until she could repeat it back to him word for word.

Satisfied that she could remember Ott's message, Kate thought a moment and then asked, "Ott, if you are my mother's husband's youngest son's youngest older brother, then who am I?"

"Well, that would make you your brother's mother's husband's youngest son's youngest oldest brother's sister, I think," replied Ott.

"Good," said Kate, giggling. "I think so too."

# 3

# Eating Iowa Dirt

"Grandma, would you tell us about when you were little, please?" asked Kate. We had gathered near the fireplace as we usually did on winter nights, after having cleaned up from supper.

"Before we have any stories," said Ma, "the bricks have to be set out. Boys?" On cold winter nights, we bundled hot bricks at the foot of each bed to help us keep warm.

"Ott and Johnny, go get the bricks," commanded Elias. "I'll stoke up the fire."

"Yes sir, General, sir," said Ott as he saluted Elias.

Ott and I retrieved the bricks from the bedrooms and placed them on the fireplace hearth, close enough to the embers to get them plenty hot. I also set a bucket of water next to the bricks.

The fire was soon blazing with bright flames, and the warmth felt good.

"Please tell us about when you were little, Grandma," said Kate, repeating her earlier request.

"Yes, please," I echoed.

"Ma," said Elias, "I'm going out to the barn to work on Mr. Burt's saddle. I told him I'd have it ready by the weekend."

"I'll help you, Elias," said Ott.

"I can do it myself. I don't need any help," said Elias.

"I'll come out anyway. You can show me how it's done," said Ott. Elias shrugged.

"Boys, take the oil lamp with you," said Ma. "The fireplace is giving us enough light for now."

After Elias and Ott left to go to the barn, Grandma chuckled and said, "I find it amazing that you young'uns are not tired of listening to my childhood tales."

"Well, your stories are exciting, Grandma," said Kate. "Just think, you lived at the same time as George Washington and Christopher Columbus and all those famous people."

"Well, George Washington, yes, for a few years, but that fellow Christopher Columbus … hmm, I'm not sure," said Grandma.

"That's too bad, Grandma. Columbus would have been a real interesting person to meet," said Kate.

"Hmm, now that I think about it, though, maybe I did see him eating dinner at an inn once. Would he have had three ships—the Nina, the Pinta, and the Santa Claus?"

"Santa Maria, Grandma," said Kate patiently. "Yes, he would have had those three ships."

"And would he have been all dressed up in funny clothing that only people from other parts of the world wear?"

"Yes, Grandma, I think so," said Kate.

"That's the guy, then," said Grandma. "Yes, he said he got lost trying to find his way to western Indiana to buy spices and he ended up at that inn in Virginia."

Kate looked at Grandma with serious eyes, as if trying to determine whether Grandma was teasing. Finally, Kate started laughing. "You did not see him at an inn, Grandma. That is silly. They didn't have inns back then."

Grandma smiled. "Kate, you are too smart for me. They didn't even have food back then, did they?"

Kate looked curiously at Grandma. "They didn't?"

"I think they invented food shortly after I turned ten."

"What did you eat before they invented food?"

"Dirt."

"Dirt?"

"Yes, but back then we had good, rich dirt, not like the dirt you find outside these days. I still eat dirt every now and then, though. It cleans out the throat."

"You do? That sounds awful, Grandma!" said Kate.

"Catherine, would you mind bringing me a spoonful of dirt?"

"I would be happy to, Mother," said Ma, smiling. Ma took a spoon and scooped it into the remnants of the cake she had attempted. Holding her hand under the spoon, she brought it to Grandma, who took it from Ma and quickly put it in her mouth.

"Root Cellar, 1876," said Ma with a twinkle in her eyes.

"Mmm, a very good year," said Grandma, still chewing.

Kate stared in amazement.

"Ma, could I have some dirt too?" I asked. Again Ma smiled, and she brought over another spoonful of the brown, crumbly stuff, and I ate it. It actually tasted pretty good. Kate watched me closely.

"How's the dirt, Johnny?" asked Ma.

"It's good, Ma, kind of earthy," I said. "Kate, you should try some."

Kate's face turned pale. "I … uh … I don't think I will right now. The thought of eating dirt makes me not feel so well. Maybe some other time. Grandma, tell us about meeting George Washington," she said, obviously trying to change the subject.

Grandma winked and then began her story. "Well, one Christmas Eve, I decided to take a walk along the Delaware River, and a boat stops alongside of me, and this gentleman in a uniform asks me for directions. Well …."

Grandma continued her stories. We listened, entranced, for about fifteen minutes, but then Grandma developed a coughing spell that would not quit.

"I think I have to stop for now," said Grandma with a sigh. We loved hearing Grandma's stories, but tomorrow always brought time for more. Besides, I felt my eyes drooping.

Just then, Elias and Ott returned from the barn. Using warm water from a bucket that we kept near the fire, we washed up to get ready for bed. Ott and I retrieved the hot bricks from the fireplace and placed a couple at the foot of each bed. Elias piled the embers and coals in the fireplace into a mound so that we would have hot coals in the morning to help start the fire. Finally, we all crawled into bed for the night.

As I lay in bed in the dark, I thought about George Washington and Christopher Columbus and the old days. It felt like times had changed, and I began wondering if any more adventures could be found, any more opportunities to be a hero. I reckoned that since I was ten years old already, I was running out of time. Restless, I tossed and turned a while, but eventually I rolled over and fell asleep, praying that adventures would come before I got too old.

# 4

# Darkness of Winter

The sound of the howling wind buffeting the walls of our little house woke me up in the morning. The cold air—I could see my breath—made me want to burrow down deep in my blankets. I scooted over toward Ott's side of the bed to put my back against his in an attempt to warm up, but I found his side empty.

Ma's voice called out. "Boys, get up. Kate, you too. It's time for morning chores. The sooner you get out there, the sooner you can come back in."

Suddenly the covers were pulled off the bed and the frigid air wrapped itself around my body. I looked up. I should have known. Ott, the prankster, stood there with a big smile and an armful of blankets.

"Up, slug-a-bed," he teased.

Cold without the blankets—and without Ott—I sat up and got out of bed. Still wearing most of my clothes from the day before—that was the best way to stay warm enough at night—I grabbed my flannel shirt and winter coat from the hook on the wall.

After bundling up, I stepped outside. The wind stung my cheeks as if someone had given my face a stiff slap, and it made my eyes tear up. Despite the brutal cold, I stopped and marveled at the beauty of the early dawn sky. With no moon to interfere, I could see some of the stars above.

Another blast of wind hit me; my muscles tensed up, trying to stay warm. Feeling bone cold, I wanted to get the chores done quickly so that we could go back inside.

The door opened and out stepped Kate, followed by Elias, and then Ott, carrying a bucket of hot water. The hardest part about doing chores in the bitter cold involved making sure the animals had enough water to drink. The water in the troughs would freeze during the night, so we used the hot water to thaw and prime the well pump, and then we pumped enough water for the animals.

We followed our usual routine that morning—Elias and I fed the horses, Millie and Billy, and the pig, Ollie; Ott milked the cow, Constance; and Kate fed the chickens. George would help with chores too, when he was there, though often in the early mornings he went to his regular job at Summey's Shoes in town.

By the time we finished our chores and headed back inside the house, the sun had lifted over the horizon. Ma had breakfast cooking on the stove. Grandma's rocking chair sat empty near the fire.

"Where's Grandma?" I asked.

"She's not well. She says her throat feels like it is on fire, and she's having a fit trying to breathe," said Ma.

Ma's father, Grandpa Shideler, had been a doctor, and Ma learned medicine from him. She knew more about herbal remedies than just about anyone else in the county.

"Let's sit down to eat," said Ma. "Ott, bring over the johnnycakes, please. Johnny, get the butter and syrup."

Ott brought over a plateful of johnnycakes, fresh from the frying pan. Johnnycakes were made with a thick cornmeal batter and fried in the skillet. I carried over the hot pitcher of sorghum syrup.

The steam rising from the johnnycakes and syrup sure felt good against my face on that cold morning. We ate quickly and in silence. We were all worried about Grandma.

After we finished eating, Ma went in the bedroom to check on Grandma. When Ma came out, she said, "We need to pray for her, children." She walked back into the bedroom, and we followed.

"Elias, would you lead us?"

Ma got down on her knees beside the bed, as did the rest of us. Elias knelt last of all.

"Dear God," Elias began, and then he paused. I waited for him to go on, but the moments passed quietly. I waited some more. Perhaps he was praying silently. I opened my eyes and looked at him, and he looked right back at me. He shrugged and then closed his eyes, but he remained silent.

Ma did not say anything at first, but then she continued the prayer. "Lord, you are the great physician and you are the comforter. We pray that you would stretch your arms down and touch Grandma, healing her and restoring her to good health. Amen."

An uncomfortable silence hovered in the air after Ma finished, and finally Kate asked what we were all thinking: "Elias, why didn't you finish the prayer?"

Elias shrugged. "I … I don't know," he stammered. "Ma, I'm going to bring in some firewood."

"Okay, Elias," said Ma, quietly. "We'll sing some hymns and do some reading for Grandma when you come back."

"You can begin without me," said Elias.

"No, we'll wait for you. That's fine," replied Ma.

A few minutes later, Elias came in with a large armload of split wood.

We gathered around Grandma's bed and took turns reading our favorite Bible passages and singing some of our favorite hymns.

When we finished singing "Holy, Holy, Holy," Grandma opened her eyes and whispered, "You sound so wonderful this morning, almost like a choir of angels."

"That is because Pa is not here, Grandma," laughed Kate. We boys nodded in agreement. Pa could do many things, but singing didn't really agree with him.

"Now Kate, be respectful," said Ma, a bit sternly but with a twinkle in her eyes.

"Yes, Ma," said Kate in obedience.

The winter winds continued shaking the house, and by late morning we could see a snowstorm over the western horizon, heading our way. Pa and George hadn't planned on getting back until the afternoon, but the longer the morning went on, the more anxious we got. I tried reading, but I couldn't concentrate. I kept wondering about them.

Ma came out of the bedroom with a smile.

"How's Grandma?" I asked.

"Doing better. She's not coughing as often and is sleeping now. I think she'll be fine," said Ma. She looked relieved.

The snow started falling by early afternoon, and as the hours passed, the apprehension about Pa and George turned into worry and then became fear.

As evening approached, Elias and Ott went outside to make sure the animals had gone into the barn for the day.

Kate turned to me and whispered, "Johnny, I'm scared about Pa and George. When are they coming home?"

"I don't know, Kate. I'm scared too."

Kate said, "Please pray with me, Johnny," but before I could respond, she closed her eyes tightly and said, "Dear God, please bring them home safely."

At that moment, the front door opened. Kate's eyes lit up brightly and she broke out into a big smile. Elias and Ott walked in, carrying more firewood. Kate's smile disappeared. She turned her downcast face away from the door, only to hear Ott say, "Look who we found wandering along the road!"

"We're home," boomed George's voice. In walked George and Pa, white with snow.

"Pa! George!" Kate giggled, running toward the door and leaping into Pa's arms.

"Kate, boys," said Pa with a happy sigh. His face was red from the cold Iowa wind. Pa and George removed their coats and went to the fireplace to warm.

"Where's Mother?" Pa asked, spying the empty rocking chair.

"Sick in bed," said Ma, "but she's on the mend."

"We've been praying for her, Pa," said Kate. "I think it's working."

"Of course it's working," said Pa with a hint of a smile.

"We've brought in extra firewood, Pa, and the animals have bedding and enough food in the barn to last a while," said Elias.

"Good," said Pa. "There's just one thing left to do then."

"What's that, Pa?" Ott asked with some amount of trepidation.

"I've got to make sure you children don't get the cholera morbus."

In the Great Rebellion, Pa had learned how to make a tonic that supposedly kept sickness away. He said it would cure everything from sore throats to something he called "cholera morbus." We didn't know what cholera morbus was, but Pa had us believing it was as bad as it sounded. At the slightest suggestion that we might be under the weather, Pa would feed us the tonic.

Taking a spoonful of tonic was like trying to swallow a lightning bolt—it burned the mouth, lips, and everything else all the way down to the stomach. A second spoonful would set the room to spinning.

"Pa, no, please, I think we'll all be okay," I whimpered.

My begging was not successful. Pa was bent on giving us his tonic, and once he decided to do something it was all but impossible to get him to change his mind.

As I lay in bed that night, I thought about cholera morbus. Then I overheard Ma telling Pa that Grandma wanted another spoonful of Pa's tonic. "But that's four spoonfuls, Catherine," I heard Pa say. Pa relented in the end and gave Grandma another spoonful.

Four spoonfuls of Pa's tonic—if it didn't kill her, it would certainly make her better.

I said another prayer for Grandma to get well, and I fell asleep thinking about warming my cheeks against Grandma's cheeks in front of the fireplace.

# 5

# Traps

"Come on, lazy boy, help me check the traps," said George, tugging on the back of my coat. We had just finished morning chores, and I wanted to go inside and warm my cold hands.

I turned and looked at George. He liked calling me lazy boy, though I knew that he knew that there wasn't a lazy bone in my body—well, most days anyway. George had a seriousness about him that belied his age. I'd forget that he was my brother; sometimes he seemed more like an uncle or a second father. He didn't strive for attention the way Elias did, but he always "got her done," as Pa would say.

"I'm cold, George."

"Me too. But there might be supper out there waiting for us, and we need to check," said George. He had a good point. We always prayed, "Give us this day our daily bread," but what good did praying do if we didn't go look to see if God had delivered?

George began walking out toward the woods where we kept two small traps. The traps would never catch anything big for us, but we got our fair share of squirrels and rabbits, along with an occasional possum or raccoon.

I turned and followed George. We walked a while in silence, and then George began whistling "Yankee Doodle." I knew George well enough to know that he didn't whistle just to make merry; he whistled so that any large animals who happened to be feasting on trapped prey might hear us and skedaddle out of there before we arrived. We wanted to avoid catching a wolf or mountain lion by surprise, and black bears had even been seen in central Iowa every once in a while.

The first trap had no game and showed no signs of being disturbed, but when we got to the second we found a rabbit. George removed it from the trap and held it up to admire.

"Yeah!" he exclaimed, "Nice and plump. It'll make a good dinner tonight."

"Ma will be happy," I said.

"Sure will," agreed George. "Now let's go home and get some breakfast."

We reset the trap and then headed across the field back toward the house. When I walked through the door, the first thing I heard was the familiar sound of Grandma's rocking chair, creaking back and forth.

"Grandma! You're up! How are you feeling this morning?" I asked.

"Never better, Johnny. I feel so good I almost can't stand it. Do you need your cheeks warmed?"

"Yes, please," I smiled. "I'm cold."

"Oh, Johnny," she said as she pressed her cheek against mine, "I love you."

"I love you too, Grandma," I said. "We were praying for you. I'm glad you're better."

"Thank you, Johnny. I'm glad too."

Later that morning, after we had eaten, Sam came over and all of us children joined in for the snowball fight to end all snowball fights.

The air felt unusually warm, and with the bright, shining sun, the snow was beginning to melt. These conditions made for perfect packing snow, and the snowballs were coming a mile a minute.

Whoopin' and hollerin', we chased each other around the house, yard, and fields, hiding behind the barn, trees, and anywhere else we could escape detection. We sometimes played in teams—changing teams often—and sometimes we went alone.

"I see you, Johnny Stevens!" yelled Sam. "Charge!" He began running toward me at full speed. I ran around the side of the house and then turned the corner.

Thinking quickly, I stepped into the old outhouse—first time I'd been in there since George and Elias built the new two-seater a couple of years ago—and closed the door, hoping Sam would think I had kept running. Listening from just inside the door, I heard his footsteps rushing past. I patted myself on the back for my brilliant maneuver.

I decided to sit down and rest to catch my breath. At the moment that my bottom hit wood, I heard a splintering sound and, before I knew what was happening, I had fallen through the seat and was wedged into the bottom of the outhouse, stuck with my head and feet at about seat-level and my bottom resting on the top of the pit.

It was my good fortune to find that the pit was both filled-in and frozen, or it could have been much worse. But still, I was stuck. I thought about calling for help.

The door suddenly opened and Ott stepped in, closing the door quickly. He was breathing hard. I waited but he said nothing. Apparently he hadn't seen me down below.

"Hey, Ott," I whispered after a few seconds.

Ott screamed and flung the outhouse door open, falling to his knees before bursting out in laughter.

"Johnny ... Johnny Stevens, boy, you scared me," gasped Ott. The others came running to see what had happened and found me stuck, rear-end first, in the old outhouse pit.

"Johnny, you're hiding down there?" asked Kate.

"No, Kate, I—"

"Johnny, are you okay?" asked Ott, still laughing.

"I … uh … I guess so," I stammered. "I'm not sure."

"Let's get you out of there," said George. He reached in and grabbed one arm, and Ott reached in and grabbed the other, and the two of them lifted me up and out.

"Well," said George, looking me over, "you don't look any worse for the wear, other than a knot on the back of your head."

"I … I'm okay," I said, more embarrassed than anything.

"You'd better be okay, Johnny, or Pa's going to make us take more of his tonic," whispered Kate.

We all laughed and then resumed the snowball fight, and before long the air was practically filled with snowballs flying east, west, and every which way.

During the heat of the battle, I noticed the root cellar door had swung open. I cautiously approached it to see if anyone was hiding down there, waiting to ambush me. Just when I reached the opening, Kate hopped out. She had a circle of what looked like dirt around her lips and she wore a horrible expression on her face. "I eed ub otter," she mumbled as she tried to wipe her tongue with her hands. I interpreted that to mean, "I need some water."

"Kate, were you eating dirt in the cellar?" I asked.

"Dirt? Uh uh," she grunted before disappearing into the house. She returned minutes later with an odd smile on her face, ready to continue the snowball fight.

Kate, Sam, and I planned an all-out attack on the others. Sam went around the corner of the barn to scout the positions of our opponents. I crouched, waiting for Sam's signal, and Kate hid right behind me with a bucket of snow. Suddenly I felt a hard tug on my coat collar and I gasped as she dumped the bucket of snow down my back!

I shouted, "Kate, why did you do that?"

She grinned. "Next time, maybe you won't tell me that chocolate spice cake is really dirt." She turned and ran the opposite direction, giggling. I deserved it.

We played until noon, ate dinner, and then spent the rest of the day helping Pa with barn repairs. The snow continued melting in the warm sun, and we took off our coats and toiled until the sunlight faded. The early evening shadows cast a peaceful, blue hue on the snow as we finished up for the day and headed back to the house.

"Feels like a June evening, doesn't it Johnny?" asked Grandma when I came back in from outside.

"Sure does, Grandma."

"January thaw! This is one of the warmest that I can remember. Yes sir, if you don't like the weather in Iowa, just wait a couple of minutes and it will change," Grandma laughed.

"Yep, Grandma, I think spring is almost here."

"Spring?" said Grandma. "Winter's not even close to being done. God's just teasing us a little."

"But it's so warm outside, Grandma."

"Johnny," Grandma said, "Iowa is one of the only places on God's green earth where you can have summer in the middle of winter and winter in the middle of summer."

"Winter in the middle of summer?" I asked.

"Have I ever told you about the time we had snow in the first week of June?"

"No, you haven't," I said.

"Well, the crops were growing, and everything was green for as far as the eye could see. The day was so nice that I had taken off my shoes, walked across the field, and was having a picnic lunch in the meadow. But the next thing I knew, in the span of maybe only a few minutes, a cold wind started howling, the skies grew cloudy, and God dropped his bucket of big, white flakes right there on top of me!"

"Grandma, you must have been cold."

"Cold? I was freezing," she laughed. "I don't think I thawed out until the middle of July."

Even though Grandma's story had told me otherwise, the possibility of spring had me itching for adventure. The thaw continued through the week, melting the snow and showing signs of an early spring. I was optimistic.

"Pa, I'm seeking some serious adventures," I said on Friday morning. "Here I am at ten years old and still have done nothing significant in my life. Any ideas?"

"Start with taking a shovel and mucking the barn stalls."

"Pa, I'm serious."

"So am I, Johnny," he said. "Being adventurous means grabbing hold of opportunity and wrestling it to the ground. You don't get opportunities by just sitting on your behind, waiting for them to show up at the door. You have to be willing to work hard and to do the tasks that nobody else wants to do. That will give you more opportunities for adventure than you can shake a stick at."

Pa handed me a shovel. "Here you go, son."

"Thanks, Pa."

I knew better than to argue. I took the shovel and stepped toward the barn. Real adventure would have to wait for another day.

# 6

# School

"Now children, please pull out your Latin assignments," said Miss Baines, standing in front of the large slate board attached to the wall behind her desk.

Miss Baines taught twenty students, first through eighth grade, in the one-room schoolhouse. There was nothing beyond eighth grade. You had to go down to Des Moines to get a high school education.

A picture of George Washington hung above the slate board, and the American flag with its thirty-seven stars stood on a pole to the right of the board. Besides our desks, the only other things in the room were a piano, which Miss Baines would play for us, and the wood stove in the back.

Miss Baines knew all about math, history, and English, and I enjoyed studying those subjects because I figured they would be useful to know.

Miss Baines also tried to teach us Latin, and Pa said we were lucky to have that opportunity. I wasn't as sure about that, and I didn't know why Caesar couldn't have just said, "And you, Brutus?" instead of, "Et tu, Brute?" Seems like things would be a whole lot easier if we all spoke one language. I asked Pa when would I ever use "Et tu, Brute" outside of school, and he pointed out that I likely would live many years after I finished school and that I never knew where I might use something that I learned. I said, "Et tu, Brute," to Mr. Ledbetter one time in his general store, but he just stared at me like I had three eyes in my head.

"Do you have any questions from the Latin assignment?" Miss Baines asked.

Kate, usually the first one to ask questions, shot her hand into the air.

"Yes, Kate?" said Miss Baines, smiling. Miss Baines liked Kate.

"Miss Baines, is Julius Caesar still alive?"

"No Kate, he died a long time ago."

Sam, sitting in the desk next to mine, leaned over and whispered, "He's dead? I didn't even know he was sick! I suppose that's what happens when you speak Latin all the time."

Sam always enjoyed trying to make me laugh. I pursed my lips and did everything I could to keep from laughing. Determined not to laugh, I could feel my face turning red.

Miss Baines glanced at Sam and me. She didn't say anything—in fact, I detected a smile. Miss Baines liked Sam and me too. We were good students and we usually paid attention in class, though once in a while our laughter got us in trouble.

Kate's hand went up again.

"Yes, Kate?" asked Miss Baines.

"Miss Baines, was Mr. Caesar very smart?"

"I suppose he was, Kate," replied Miss Baines.

"How come he didn't speak English then?" asked Kate.

"I don't think English as we know it had really been invented yet."

"Oh," said Kate, thinking about that answer a moment. "Miss Baines?"

"Yes, Kate?"

"Who invented English?"

"Well, it wasn't really invented by one person."

"You mean a whole country just decided to change its language?"

"Well, it doesn't quite work that way, but—"

"Miss Baines?"

"Yes, Kate?"

"Will somebody tell us if the United States is going to change its language?"

"I hope so, Kate."

"Me too, Miss Baines."

On the way home from school, Sam, Kate, and I were walking together. "Johnny," began Kate, "if somebody changes our language, what would they change it to?"

"I don't know, Kate."

Sam said, "Maybe they would let the three of us pick the language, or maybe we could even invent a new one."

Kate smiled excitedly. "I hope they ask us! That would be fun to make a whole new language."

"What would you call that thing, in your new language?" asked Sam, pointing at a tree.

"I might call it a 'barker' because it has bark on it," replied Kate.

"Then what would you call a dog?" asked Sam.

"I might call it a 'tailer' because it has a tail," she said.

"Then what would you call a person who makes clothing?" Sam asked.

"I might call that person a 'warmer' because he would help keep us warm."

"Then what word would you use when something is not as cold as before?"

"I might use … oh, I might use 'warmer' for that too. Making our own language will be hard."

"I think so too, Kate," I agreed.

"Me too," admitted Sam.

We walked a while further.

"Johnny," said Kate, "I hope they don't ask us to invent a language."

"I don't think they will, Kate."

She seemed relieved, but I could tell she was still thinking about it. That night, after supper, she asked, "Pa? Did anyone ever ask you to invent a language?"

Pa looked at her and said, "No, nobody has asked me that, Kate."

"That's good, Pa. You're probably old enough that if somebody was going to ask you to invent a language, it would have already happened by now."

"You're right, Kate. Has somebody asked you to come up with a new language?"

"No sir," said Kate.

"Well," said Pa, "If you have to create a new language someday, I'm sure it would be a good one."

"I don't know, Pa. It's hard coming up with new words. I kind of like the words we already have."

"Me too, Kate."

# 7

# Sundays

"Up, boys. It's church day," said Ma in her Sunday morning voice.

I rubbed the sleep from my eyes. Sometimes I had trouble accepting the fact that the Lord's day of rest didn't mean that I could get a little extra rest myself. Life on the farm didn't work that way. The animals needed to be fed on Sundays, the same as any other day, and if no one fed them, well, they went hungry.

I rolled off of my side of the bed, grabbed my clothes from the hook, got dressed in the crowded room—Ott, Elias, and George were also up and getting dressed—and then stepped outside.

The early January morning sky, crisp and deep blue, was warm. The thaw continued, and our boots squished in the soft mud as we walked to the barn.

"I'll go up and get the hay, Elias," I said, climbing up the ladder to the hay loft in the barn. I grabbed armfuls of hay and tossed them into a hole in the hay loft floor above the food trough.

After finishing chores and then breakfast, we climbed into the back of the wagon for the twenty-minute ride to the Polk City United Brethren Church.

When we arrived, we found Reverend and Mrs. Jacobs at the door, greeting people as they entered the church. Reverend Jacobs' eyes twinkled as he shook my hand and said, "A blessed morning to you, Johnny."

I tried to slip behind Pa and go unnoticed by Mrs. Jacobs. I liked her and everything—I mean, she was always so nice to us children—but she gave a hug to each person walking through that door every Sunday, and her hugs were not normal hugs. She hugged like she was trying to squeeze the air out of a bull.

"Johnny!" boomed Mrs. Jacobs.

"Good morning, Mrs. Jacobs," I said politely. I stuck out my arm as though I intended to shake her hand.

"What's this? A handshake? You're a silly one today, Johnny." With that, she hugged me so hard I thought my eyeballs were going to pop out.

"God bless you, Johnny Stevens," she said, ruffling my hair with her hands.

We sat in our usual spot, the fourth row back on the left side. Pa normally would not have objected to sitting in the first or second row, but the Skinner family sat in the third row, and Mr. Skinner sang even more off-key than Pa did.

"Morning, John, Catherine," said Mr. Shanley as he and Mrs. Shanley settled into the row behind us. He reached out and patted me on the back. Mr. Shanley, the landlord of our farm, let us stay there for a very reasonable rent, according to Pa. Pa told me once that Mr. Shanley, without a doubt, was the nicest man on the face of the earth.

We sang a couple of hymns, said some prayers, and passed around the offering plate, and then Reverend Jacobs stepped into the pulpit.

"What would you do," said Reverend Jacobs as he began the sermon, "if one of your animals out in the farm yard said something to you? I am not talking about a moo or an oink or a cluck; I am talking about an animal telling you that you need to plant your seeds or that you need to fix that hole in the roof before it rains again."

He paused and let this sink in, his eyes twinkling. "You probably would give your head a shake or two, thinking you were imagining things. You might wonder about that cup of coffee that you drank at breakfast." He smiled, amused at that thought.

Kate leaned forward, riveted in her seat. She seemed to be savoring every word that rolled off of Reverend Jacobs' tongue.

"Well," continued Reverend Jacobs, "the Bible tells us in the Old Testament about a man named Balaam who traveled on his donkey to see some men that God did not want him to see. Three times, God put an angel on the path with the intent of punishing Balaam. Three times the donkey saw the angel and left the path to protect Balaam. And three times Balaam beat the donkey because he had left the path. Finally the donkey, tired of getting struck by his master, stopped and asked why Balaam continued to beat him. That certainly got Balaam's attention. Would it get yours? Well, sometimes God speaks to us in mysterious ways."

Through the entire sermon, Kate, eyes wide and mouth agape, seemed fascinated with the preacher's message about Balaam's talking donkey. I, on the other hand, had trouble concentrating on the sermon. The thaw caused me to think about the possibility of an early spring, which meant that I could go fishing soon, and I started dreaming about all the big fish in the creek that were just waiting to be caught. Besides that, I was hungry, and my stomach kept growling and making noises. I wanted to go home, talking donkey or not.

"Now," said Reverend Jacobs, "before we conclude our service, there is something I must do. One member of the congregation seems to be particularly interested in today's message, and I am suitably impressed due to the young age of this person. I don't normally hand out rewards when I catch someone actually listening to my sermons, but I am feeling led to break with my routine today."

He walked over to our pew and handed Kate a small bag.

"Kate Stevens, this bag of licorice candy is for you. I am glad that you seemed to enjoy today's sermon, and I hope that you enjoy the licorice." Kate beamed with pride, but my stomach could only growl in response.

After we returned home and ate our big Sunday dinner, I noticed Kate quietly slip out the door. She was up to something. I sneaked out and followed her around to the side yard, where she sat down in front of Old Jack. I hid behind the big oak tree in the side yard.

"God, do you have anything to say to me?" Kate looked hopefully at Old Jack.

Old Jack wagged his tail.

"God, I know you're in there."

Old Jack leaned forward and licked Kate on the nose.

"God, if you have a message for me, I'm listening, I'm right here, now is your chance."

Old Jack looked at Kate quizzically.

"I promise, God, that I won't beat up Old Jack like Balaam beat up his talking donkey. God, please say something."

After a couple of moments of silence, I decided that I couldn't pass up this opportunity.

I whispered, "Kate."

Kate just about jumped out of her skin.

"God ... God, is that you?" she stammered.

"Kate, give Johnny some licorice," I whispered.

Then she turned around and saw me.

"Why, you …" and she tackled me, knocking me over, and began tickling me in the ribs. I was laughing so hard that I couldn't fight back. Old Jack joined in the fray, yelping and licking my face.

Pa called out from the house. "Are you two okay? I heard some noise."

I sat up. "Yes sir, just playing with my little sister Balaam."

Pa smiled. "Trying to get Old Jack to talk?"

Kate spoke up. "Yes sir, if a donkey could do it, Old Jack can. He's smarter than any donkey I've ever seen."

"Well you know, in Old Testament Bible times, they were really speaking in Hebrew. Maybe animals don't speak English," said Pa.

"I never thought of that," Kate admitted.

For the rest of the afternoon, Kate walked Old Jack around the yard and down by the creek, trying to teach him words. She even convinced me to help, after giving me two pieces of licorice. At the end of the day, I figured that Old Jack didn't have the desire to learn English. He seemed to be content speaking his own language.

Kate, however, was not content with that. "Johnny," she said, "I have an idea."

"What is it, Kate?"

"You'll find out at school tomorrow," she grinned.

# 8

# Learning Hebrew

Kate raised her hand.

"Yes, Kate?" asked Miss Baines.

"Miss Baines, could we learn Hebrew today instead of Latin?"

"Hebrew?"

"You know, the Bible language that they used in the Old Testament. It seems like that would be really useful to learn."

"Oh, it would be most useful, indeed. There's just one small problem."

"What's that?"

"I don't know Hebrew."

An awkward moment of silence filled the air. Kate appeared to be surprised that a teacher might not know everything.

"Miss Baines?"

"Yes, Kate?"

"Did you go all the way through school, or did you have to stop short because your family needed help on the farm?"

Miss Baines smiled. "I went all the way through school, Kate. Now, we need to get on with the day's lessons."

And so class began. Kate didn't argue, and she didn't say more about it while we were at school, but I could see the wheels spinning in her mind. Unusually quiet on the walk home that afternoon, Kate still seemed troubled by the revelation that a teacher might not know everything.

"What's on your mind, Kate?"

"I'm thinking about Miss Baines. Do you think she has something wrong with her brain?"

"Why do you say that?"

"Well, she finished schooling but doesn't remember Hebrew—and she doesn't remember even learning Hebrew."

"Kate, you don't learn everything in school."

"Well, where would you learn Hebrew if you don't learn it in school?"

"Not all schools teach the same things."

"They don't?"

"They can't. There's so much to learn. I mean, think about it. Even with languages, there's English and Spanish and Latin and Hebrew and Chinese and a bunch of others probably. Some of them use different alphabets, and some of them don't even have alphabets."

"How do you know that?"

"Pa told me once."

"Pa knows a lot."

"Yep, he does. So does Ma."

"Johnny, how come Ma and Pa don't know Hebrew?"

"How do we know that they don't know Hebrew?"

"I think," said Kate, "that if they knew Hebrew, we would hear them talking with Old Jack."

Good point," I said. "I guess that makes sense. Maybe they knew Hebrew but just forgot."

"Maybe. Johnny, how old is Miss Baines?"

"I don't know, Kate. She's pretty old though, maybe twenty-four or twenty-five."

"She should know Hebrew by now, don't you think?"

"Maybe, Kate," I agreed, just to get Kate to stop talking about it.

"We'll have to pray for her, Johnny, that she'll learn Hebrew and that she'll get well if something is wrong with her."

I smiled. "I don't think anything is wrong with her, Kate. She's just busy, that's all." Kate seemed relieved with that.

"Johnny, I have an idea."

"What's that, Kate?"

"The next time we go in to town, we could stop at Ledbetter's and see if they have any books on how to learn Hebrew."

"That's a great idea, Kate," I said. "Ledbetter's doesn't have a lot of books, but it seems like a book on Hebrew would be one of them."

When we said our family prayers that night, Kate added, "And please, God, help Miss Baines finish her learning so that she can teach us Hebrew before we get too old."

# 9

# Ledbetter General Store

"Well, if it isn't John and Johnny Stevens," said Mr. Rafe Ledbetter as Pa and I entered his general store in Polk City on a Saturday morning, coming out of the bright light of the blue sky and into the dimly lit room. It took my eyes a moment to adjust to the shadows. I noticed Sheriff Cogswell, a hulk of a man with a booming laugh and tough but friendly eyes, studying the checkerboard on the counter. Apparently there was a game in progress.

"Morning, John," Mr. Ledbetter said to Pa. "Johnny," he said, nodding toward me.

"Hello, Mr. Ledbetter," I replied.

"Good morning, Rafe, Sheriff," added Pa. Sheriff Cogswell nodded.

"John, you're growing up to look like your son a bit more every day," Mr. Ledbetter said with a wink. "What can I get for you today?"

"I need a couple pounds of fence nails, and I've got a list here from the missus," said Pa, handing a piece of paper to Mr. Ledbetter.

"That's the game, Rafe," said Sheriff Cogswell as he used one of his red kings to jump Mr. Ledbetter's three remaining black pieces. "I've got to head out," said the sheriff, before stopping mid-stride to look at me. He smiled. "Johnny, you're an inch taller every time I see you." He turned toward Pa and said, "John, you're raising your young'uns right. We need more of 'em like the Stevens children."

"Thanks, Sheriff," said Pa, nodding as Sheriff Cogswell left the store.

I walked around the store while Mr. Ledbetter filled the order. The fragrances from containers of coffee, tobacco, chocolate, and cinnamon—and especially the pickle barrel—wafted throughout the store, mingling with the aromas of new cotton cloth and leather belts and shoes. My nose tickled from the scent of peppery spices and burned from the pungent odor of soaps, both at the same time.

Mr. Ledbetter always displayed new gadgets on the front counter, and I enjoyed trying to guess what they were. He constantly tried to find unique, innovative products to sell, whether some newfangled invention or an unusual and exotic food. As a result, his store didn't always do too well—he carried some things on his shelves that the average person in Polk City, Iowa, just didn't have the need to buy. He had a friendly demeanor though, and everybody in town liked him.

"Pa, can we get some dried peaches?"

"Sure, Johnny."

I walked over to the barrel where Mr. Ledbetter kept the dried peaches, and met a surprise. Mr. Ledbetter's cat, Mrs. Lincoln, lay inside the barrel on top of the peaches as she nursed six newborn kittens.

"Mr. Ledbetter, did you know Mrs. Lincoln has herself a new home, hiding out in the peach barrel? Looks like she's got some kittens."

"So that's where she's gone to," said Mr. Ledbetter, walking over to the barrel and peeking in. Shaking his head, he sighed and said, "More mouths to feed." He pulled an empty wooden box out from behind the counter, placed the kittens in it—at the objection of a disagreeable Mrs. Lincoln—and carried the box of kittens to the far corner, in the shadows, where they could have some peace and quiet.

Mr. Ledbetter returned to the barrel of dried peaches, looked inside, and pulled out three or four slices. With the shadows in the store making it difficult to see down into the barrel, I don't know how Mr. Ledbetter knew which peach slices to remove. He poked around in the barrel a little more, pulled out two more slices, and threw them into the waste basket.

"Now, how much would you like, Johnny?" he asked, motioning to the peaches.

"Um, can I get dried apples instead?" I wasn't excited about eating anything out of the peach barrel at the moment.

"Yes sir, we can do that. Allow me to scoop for you. How much would you like?"

"One scoop, please."

Mr. Ledbetter scooped the dried fruit into a small bag and handed it to me. "Here you go," he said with a smile.

"Thanks, Mr. Ledbetter! Oh, do you have any books on learning Hebrew?"

"Learning Hebrew? Uh, no, we don't," he said.

I heard the door open and I looked up only to see Clarence Slaughter standing there. My heart sank. About a year older and maybe half-a-head taller than me, Clarence meant trouble. I've heard people say that you grow up to look like your name. Well, Clarence Slaughter looked like his name even before he had finished growing up. Even worse, he acted like his name. He didn't go to school. He just liked hanging around the schoolyard and beating us up.

"Morning, Johnny Stevens," said Clarence with a sneer, and his face broke into a menacing grin that sent a shudder up my spine. Then he saw Pa, and his smile vanished. With Pa around, Clarence couldn't be the tough bully he usually was.

"Morning, Clarence," I said in as cheerful a voice as I could muster. I wanted to show him that I wasn't scared—or maybe I wanted to show Pa—but either way I had probably said the wrong thing. Clarence gave me a mean look.

He walked over to the barrels of dried fruit, where I still stood. No one else in the store could see his face, and the look in his eyes scared me.

Leaning over into the barrel of dried peaches, he whispered, "I'm gonna whoop you next chance I get, Johnny Stevens," as he used his hand to scoop maybe a half pound of the dried fruit into a bag.

"Clarence," I began, intending to tell him that he might not want to eat the peaches.

"Better keep your eyes open, Johnny Stevens," he hissed. "I'm coming after you."

I wanted to ignore his words. "Clarence, I wouldn't—"

"Wouldn't what?" he interrupted. "Wouldn't say those things right here with your father in the store? Are you going to run home crying to your mama? Well you listen to this—I'm going to squash you so flat they won't be able to scrape you off the trail to school. See you, Johnny."

He turned around and carried the bag of dried peaches to the counter. He dug his hand into his pocket, apparently trying to find coins, and then he said to Mr. Ledbetter, "Looks like I forgot my money, Mr. Ledbetter. Can I put this on my father's bill?"

"You sure that's okay with your pa?" asked Mr. Ledbetter.

"Yeah, I'm sure," said Clarence.

"All right then. Oh, one other thing. Next time, ask me for a scoop. I don't want people using their hands with the dried fruit," said Mr. Ledbetter.

"Okay, Mr. Ledbetter," said Clarence, rolling his eyes.

Clarence picked up the bag and walked to the door without even saying thank you, and when he opened it he turned and looked at me. Then he popped a dried peach slice into his mouth and walked away.

Before the door had closed all the way, it opened again and in walked Mr. Horace Kilpatrick. Mr. Kilpatrick, wearing what he always wore—white shirt, black pants, black jacket, black top hat, and carrying a cane—ran the local bank in town. His dark, beady eyes always reminded me of a snake. I never got a good look at his tongue, but it wouldn't have surprised me to find it forked.

While Clarence Slaughter played the bully who beat us up in the schoolyard, Mr. Kilpatrick hid like a serpent lying in the grass, waiting for the next unsuspecting adult victim to come near. I heard that grown men would shudder when they saw Mr. Kilpatrick coming down the street. I know that Mr. Kilpatrick didn't scare Pa—nobody scared my pa—but I don't think Pa particularly liked him either. I heard Mr. Kilpatrick didn't have many friends. It seemed to me that not having friends would be a good sign to a person that he should rethink how he does things, but it also seemed to me that adults didn't worry as much about having friends as we children did.

"Morning, Horace," said Pa, acknowledging Mr. Kilpatrick.

"Stevens, Ledbetter," said Mr. Kilpatrick. He didn't bother saying anything to me. "It's a glorious day, oh my, it's a glorious day."

"Glorious?" said Mr. Ledbetter.

"It's simply glorious. It's a glorious day any time money just falls into your lap."

Mr. Kilpatrick stood there in silence, smiling, obviously waiting for Pa or Mr. Ledbetter to ask about this money that fell in his lap. I tried to imagine riding down the street in the wagon and having a bag of money drop from the sky.

Mr. Kilpatrick continued. "Yes, indeed. It's unfortunate for Herrman but fortunate for me."

"Joseph Herrman?" asked Pa.

"The same. As they say, one man's misfortune is another man's gain," he snickered. "Joseph Herrman's farm is now mine, all mine. He missed a payment, and the bank has taken the farm. It's a glorious day, indeed."

Silence filled the room. Mr. Ledbetter said nothing. Pa said nothing either. What could they say?

"Yes, indeed, Herrman is leaving town. It is too bad really—he seemed like a decent fellow," said Mr. Kilpatrick. "Now, what was it I ... oh yes, of course. Rafe, I'd like a couple pounds of your dried peaches before I go."

"Yes sir," said Mr. Ledbetter. "They're a popular item today." He scooped the peaches into a bag and handed it to Mr. Kilpatrick, who popped a peach slice into his mouth. "Good peaches, Ledbetter. Good peaches."

I didn't say anything.

"Good day, gentlemen. Good day," said Mr. Kilpatrick, and he began whistling "Dixie" as he walked out the front door of Ledbetter's General Store.

"That man aggravates me to no end, John," sighed Mr. Ledbetter. "If I didn't owe him money, I'd give him a good shaking. That man's got some evil ideas."

Pa didn't respond right away, but he stood there scratching his chin. "Rafe, I don't know what's going on in Horace's head, but sometimes I think the good Lord puts people like that in our paths as sort of an opportunity, maybe a test, or a chance to show us how we need to depend on him."

"Oh, I suppose you are right, John. I just don't have that patience."

"I'm not sure I do either, Rafe. Maybe that's the point."

Pa paid for the goods and we headed out the door, driving home in silence.

# 10

# Neighbors

Sunday morning came again. The weather had turned cold during the night, and, waking with a shiver, I huddled for a few moments beneath the warm blankets, dreading the inevitable embrace of the chilly air. Finally deciding to get up, I stretched my arms and rolled over, accidentally slapping Ott in the face. Ott groaned, "Hey, would you milk the cow for me this morning? I want a few more minutes of sleep."

"Well, I would be willing, but you know what Pa would say."

"I know, I know. I'll get up."

Ott sat up, turned toward me, and immediately his face made an exaggerated smile. He hopped out of bed, started dancing a jig, and he made up a song that went something like this:

> Today I get to milk the cow,
> And then I'll wash and scrub the sow.
> The one says oink, the other moo,
> Then here's what I will do to you.
> I'll ... put ...
> Snakes in your socks and turtles in your pants,

*And in your hair I'll throw a bunch of ants.*
*I'll take green paint and color all your teeth,*
*And your grin will look like a Christmas wreath.*

"Sounds like you had better get up, Johnny. I think Ott has evil plans for you otherwise," laughed Pa, standing in the doorway. "Johnny," Pa added, "you and Ott can do Kate's chores this morning too. She is going to help Ma in the kitchen."

"Okay, Pa," I said. "I'll gather the eggs, Ott, if you feed the chickens."

I dressed, grabbed my overcoat, and we boys went quickly outside. I think Ott's little song and dance had put me in a happy mood. Forgetting to bring the basket with me, I put all the eggs—there were ten—in my coat pockets.

Ma and Kate had breakfast ready for us as soon as we walked in the door, so we sat down to eat. They had made cornmeal mush, and with sorghum syrup I could think of nothing more delicious on a cold winter morning. We finished eating, and then we cleaned up and headed in the wagon to church.

"A blessed day to you, Stevens family," called out Mrs. Jacobs as we walked up the steps to church that Sunday. I thought I heard bones snap when she gave me her customary hug, but I did a quick inventory afterward and I seemed to be intact.

"Where's Reverend Jacobs?" I asked.

"Oh, he's up in Cedar Rapids for the next couple of weeks, working on getting a new church started." Then quickly, to counter the look of surprise in my eyes, she added, "No, we're not leaving you—we would never do that—but he is helping out that community. We have a guest preacher from Chicago today, on his way to Omaha or some such place out west."

We took our customary seats on the left side, fourth row back. The guest preacher, thumbing through the hymnal, sat in a chair off to the side of the altar. When he finally stood up, he towered over the congregation. A bear of a man, he wrapped his large hands around the front corners of the pulpit, leaned forward, and looked each of us in the eye. He opened with a prayer. I expected to hear a booming voice that shouted out words of fire and brimstone— we had heard that kind of preacher before—but this man spoke in a soft voice, a thoughtful voice, a voice that reminded me of someone who tried to listen to God more than he tried to tell God what to do.

As soon as the prayer had ended, Elias whispered to me, "Johnny, you're dripping."

I looked down and saw a large drop of bright yellow egg yolk fall from my pocket onto the pew, joining four or five other bright yellow drops that had already fallen. In horror I realized that I had forgotten about the eggs. Some of them must have been damaged when Mrs. Jacobs hugged me.

I opened my right pocket and looked—all the eggs were broken.

I opened my left pocket and looked—same thing on that side. I sat there, watching drops from the eggs occasionally fall to the pew. My coat seemed to be soaking up most of it, which I guess was a good thing. Kate noticed it too, and she became enamored with the whole ordeal.

She whispered to Ma, who turned to me with a look of surprise. Ma then whispered to Pa, who also turned and looked. At that point, Pa began coughing. I could tell that he wanted to laugh. He reached over and squeezed my shoulder, which meant that I shouldn't worry about the eggs.

Even with that distraction, I paid attention to the church service once things really got going. The preacher gave a fine sermon that seemed to come from the heart. With a twinkle in his eye, like someone who woke up on Christmas morning and found a big present with his name on it underneath the Christmas tree, he preached about loving our neighbor and how we should not seek revenge when our neighbor does something wrong to us. After the first twenty minutes of his sermon, when most preachers started winding down, it seemed like this preacher had found his rhythm. I began to wonder if they paid him one set amount or if he got paid per word. If the latter, I reasoned, the sermon might not end for quite a while.

The preacher got to a stopping point and invited us to sing along with him. We sang, "O for a Thousand Tongues," one of Mr. Skinner's favorites. Even sitting behind Mr. Skinner, I could hear him belt out the tune. The preacher obviously could hear him too, because he stopped us after only the first verse, saying, "I believe that will suffice." I figured that we had just sung the closing hymn. My thoughts turned from church to food, and I started dreaming about the baked chicken and potato salad that Ma had made the night before in preparation for our Sunday dinner. I knew it would be good. Just thinking about it made my mouth water.

I shut my eyes, waiting for the closing benediction, but then the preacher stepped back into the pulpit, and with a shout, he said, "Did you like the warm-up act? I'm fired up now." The song hadn't been the final hymn after all, just a breather and a chance to stretch our legs.

The preacher continued by asking, "Do we have any prayer requests today?" The congregation remained silent. This wasn't the usual order that we followed in our church service, and I think it took people by surprise. The preacher patiently asked again, "Is there anything on your minds today?"

Kate's arm shot up in the air.

"Yes ma'am," the preacher said, pointing to Kate. "What are you concerned about this morning?"

"Eggs," answered Kate.

"Eggs?" echoed the preacher.

"Yes, eggs," Kate replied.

I think the preacher hoped that Kate would provide more detail. "Is there, uh, anything in particular about eggs that should be in our prayers?"

"The broken ones," Kate smiled.

The preacher returned the smile, said thank you, and began the prayer. Sure enough, during the prayer he included Kate's request. "And Lord, we pray for all the broken eggs out there, that you would continue to provide new ones for our nourishment and health." That seemed to satisfy Kate.

Even that wasn't the end of the church service, though. The preacher opened up his Bible and continued preaching. "You will recall, of course, the miracle of Jesus feeding the five thousand with just five loaves of bread and two fish. Well, after Jesus fed the five thousand, the disciples got into a boat on the Sea of Galilee while Jesus went onto the hillside to pray. Perhaps the disciples were anticipating a relaxing sail across the sea, enjoying the sunset of a splendid day featuring a spectacular miracle. I don't know. But I do know that, instead of a tranquil outing on the water, a storm came up, yes it did!"

Excitement seemed to fill the preacher with new life, like a kettle of water on the stove when it begins boiling. The preacher's eyes got a little bigger and his voice went a bit higher.

"A storm with buffeting winds came up, and the disciples were straining against their oars. What did Jesus do? Jesus walked out toward them—on the water. When they saw Jesus walking on the water, they were terrified, even though Jesus, that very day, had fed five thousand men with just five loaves of bread and two fish. Yes indeed, Jesus had just that day performed this astounding miracle, and yet the Gospel of Mark tells us that when the disciples saw Jesus walking on the water, they weren't just worried, they were terrified."

The preacher paused. Not a sound could be heard in the congregation.

"Ponder this. The very same day, the very same day that Jesus fed the five thousand—an amazing miracle—the disciples saw Jesus performing yet another miracle—walking on the water—and it terrified the daylights out of them. It terrified them, but they didn't need to be scared because they had Jesus. They had Jesus right there with them." The preacher paused to let that sink in.

"They had Jesus right there with them," the preacher repeated. "Do I hear an amen?"

The congregation made no sound.

"Do I hear an amen?" he asked again.

Again, silence prevailed.

The preacher walked down the aisle and stopped in the fourth row, right next to Kate. Kate stared intently at him.

"Little girl, would you kindly tell me your name?" the preacher asked.

"My name is Kate, sir," she replied.

"Do I hear an amen?"

Kate squeezed her eyes tightly and appeared to be concentrating really hard on something.

"Well, do I?" he asked again.

"I didn't hear an amen," she said. "Maybe it's just your stomach growling."

The congregation burst into laughter. Kate's face turned beet red. She looked confused and embarrassed.

The preacher smiled. "Miss Kate, can I get you to say an amen?"

Kate said, "Yes sir," and then she pursed her lips shut.

"Well, will you say it?" he asked, again smiling.

"Amen," she said meekly.

"Thank you, Miss Kate. Now how about the rest of you? Can I get an amen?"

"Amen," said the congregation in unison. That seemed to satisfy the preacher.

"So the disciples were terrified, even though they had just witnessed two tremendous miracles and even though Jesus joined them out there on the sea. Now, to me that sounds a whole lot like us."

The congregation adamantly clung to its silence. The preacher apparently wanted another amen. Kate squirmed in her seat.

The preacher, undaunted, continued. "I take it that you all are not used to saying 'amen' in the middle of the sermon. That's certainly okay. The point I am trying to make in this message is that if we can trust in him for the big things, is it not true that we can trust in him for the little things too? Either we believe who God says he is and we trust him, or we don't. Pick one. You cannot have it both ways." As he said this, he pounded his fist on the pulpit.

Then, in a quiet voice, he continued. "This same God who works miracles, this same God who takes care of the tiny details in our lives, this same God who is right there with us, tells us that we need to love our neighbors. When he tells us to love our neighbors, why do we think it isn't important? Look what Jesus did for us, and look what he is asking us to do for him. If loving your neighbor were not important, why does the Bible spend so much time talking about it?"

The preacher went on for a while longer before finally ending, but by then I had pretty much finished listening, and I began thinking about what would happen when I walked to school the next morning. That evening, after we finished our supper chores, I sat down next to Pa.

"Pa?"

"What is it, Johnny?"

"Pa, is Clarence Slaughter my neighbor?"

"Well son, if you mean in the Biblical sense, what do you think?"

"I see it like this. He doesn't live right next to us."

"No one lives right next to us, Johnny, except maybe the Hudsons. We're on a farm."

"And I only see Clarence maybe once each week."

"How big is this world, Johnny?"

"Miss Baines says it's about 25,000 miles around, Pa."

"So it's huge."

"It's huge."

"How far away do you think Clarence lives from us?"

"I don't know, maybe four miles?"

"When you look at the world from God's perspective, where you're looking at all 25,000 miles at the same time, do four miles seem like a long ways or is it pretty short?"

"I guess it's short, from God's perspective."

"So is Clarence your neighbor?"

"I reckon he is, Pa."

"I reckon so too, son."

I went to sleep that night thinking about Clarence. I didn't want to admit it, but I think Pa got it right. If I couldn't treat Clarence the way Jesus said to treat a neighbor—if I couldn't love Clarence the way Jesus said to love a neighbor—then why bother with trying to be a Christian?

I figured I had my work cut out for me, but if I could be nice to Clarence, I could probably be nice to just about anybody. That seemed awfully hard, though, because I knew what awaited me on the way to school the next morning.

# 11

# Clarence

The next morning found a powdery blanket of snow covering the ground. The cold, crisp air smelled fresh and alive. I should have been happy, but my heart carried a heavy weight.

During our chores, I asked Elias, "Are you needin' to go see Mr. Burt about any saddle work he has for you?" George had already left for work at Mr. Summey's store, but I was hoping that one of my other big brothers would help keep Clarence at arm's length.

"No. Pa needs Ott and me to help build a fence. Why?"

"Could you walk with Kate and me to school?"

"Walk you to school? You're ten years old, you can walk yourself."

"I don't need you to carry me, Elias. It's just that …."

"What?"

"I think Clarence Slaughter is going to come after me this morning."

"Are you scared of Clarence?"

I didn't say anything. I knew Elias wouldn't approve of me being scared of anybody.

"Besides, Sam will be with you," Elias continued.

"Sam isn't coming to school today. His pa needs him on the farm."

"Well, even so, just stand your ground, Johnny. If he beats you up, he beats you up. It's all part of growing and becoming tough."

"Thanks, Elias," I grumbled.

"Don't mention it," he smiled.

So, after finishing chores and breakfast, Kate and I went on our way to school.

Rounding the corner after about the first mile, I saw a figure standing maybe one hundred yards ahead. It was Clarence Slaughter. Kate said under her breath, "Johnny, there's trouble ahead."

I turned around and started walking back toward home.

"Johnny, where are you going?" Kate grabbed my arm and pulled me to a stop.

"Home."

"Why?"

"I'm not feeling well all of a sudden."

"Are you afraid of Clarence?"

"No."

"You are not telling the truth."

"You're right. I really don't want to see him."

"Johnny, what's the worst that can happen?"

"Oh, I don't know, death maybe?"

"I don't think Clarence will kill you. That's just my guess though."

"Well, I feel comforted now, Kate. I think he'd love to try."

"Come on."

Reluctantly, I walked with Kate. I wanted to walk behind her, but that would make me look like a coward. So I kept walking, mostly beside Kate.

"Look, let's just keep walking to school. We'll ignore him and see if he goes away." I did say a quick prayer, under my breath, for God to send down an angel of protection.

"Well, if it ain't little Johnny Stevens. Isn't that sweet, he's walking with his sister to school. Morning, Kate. Morning, Johnny."

"Morning, Clarence," Kate and I both managed to say in unison. We picked up our pace and hoped we could just keep walking.

"Why the big hurry? Don't you want to stay and talk with your friend Clarence?" He stepped in front of us, blocking our path.

Before I could respond, Clarence leaned forward and pushed me hard. My feet slipped on the ice and down I went. As I lay there in the snow, I wished I could somehow just disappear, melting into the ground. I didn't want to get back up because I knew Clarence wasn't finished with me.

"Is he dead?" Clarence asked, mockingly. "No, I don't think so. I think this boy just doesn't want to play with me."

I stood up, red faced and flustered, but the words from the preacher's sermon came back to me.

"What's the matter, Johnny? Don't know what to say? Well, let's try this again, and maybe you'll think of something to say this time."

I really didn't want to fight Clarence, so I kept my arms down.

He punched me in the face, and down I went. Part of me wanted so badly to punch him right back, but I knew both God and Pa would be happier if I didn't. Besides, the thought of hitting him scared me—that would make him mad, causing him to hit me with even more force.

Kate, however, apparently couldn't just stand there watching the events unfold. Dropping her books, she surprised Clarence with a punch that caught him in the stomach, and when he doubled over she threw another punch to his cheek, just below his left eye, sending him sprawling in the snow. Kate didn't stop there. She jumped on Clarence and continued punching him with several more licks to the stomach and chest.

"You quit?" asked Kate, teeth clenched and demanding an answer.

"I quit, I quit," moaned a defeated Clarence.

"Hey, what's this?" Kate asked, picking up a small leather pouch lying on the ground.

"That's mine, that's my money," shouted Clarence. "Give it to me!" He grabbed the pouch from her hands and ran off. He didn't look back. He had been whipped by my little sister and he knew it.

"Johnny, your eye is swelling," said Kate. She reached down, made a snowball, and handed it to me. "Here, put this on your eye. It'll help make the swelling go away."

I held the snowball to my eye. Kate picked up our books, and we continued to school.

"Kate?"

"What, Johnny?"

"Do you believe in angels?"

"Why not? The Bible talks about them. That's good enough for me."

"Me too. Kate, when we saw Clarence, I prayed an angel would protect us."

Kate chewed on that a moment. "Maybe an angel did protect us, Johnny."

"Maybe. Or maybe God helped you to be an angel for a little while."

Kate smiled. "I like that thought, Johnny."

By the time we got to school, my eye had puffed up and turned purple, and everybody—including the teacher—asked what happened.

Kate blurted out, "Clarence Slaughter ambushed us on our way here, but Johnny stood his ground and attacked back, defending me."

"Kate," I began, but then I thought better of responding. I didn't know what punishment I might receive for the fight, but I didn't want Kate to get in trouble and have to bear the brunt of any punishment, especially after she had acted so bravely.

Miss Baines scolded me lightly and said she would hold me accountable to not let my temper get out of control, even if I did not start the fight. I merely nodded and accepted the reprimand.

It was a bit different at home that night.

Pa had been in town during the afternoon and returned home just when Ma announced that dinner was ready. At the supper table, Pa broke the customary silence by asking the question, "How did things go at school today?" He had not said anything about my bruised eye, but I figured I had better tell him what happened.

I answered first. "Pa, I had a fight with Clarence Slaughter. I am sorry."

Pa sat for a moment before responding. "I ran into Clarence's father in town and heard a little about this. Did you forget what you learned in the sermon about turning the other cheek?"

"Pa," Kate interrupted, "may I say something?"

"Yes, Kate?"

"Johnny has not told you everything. Clarence pushed Johnny. Johnny got up. Clarence then punched him. Johnny never hit Clarence."

"Oh? Then who did?"

"I did, Pa. You know that Bible verse that talks about loving someone so much that you would lay down your life for that person? Well, I decided I needed to lay down my life for my brother."

"Kate, did that verse really go through your mind at that moment?"

Kate thought about it a few seconds. Her mouth twisted one way and then the other, as though she were deciding whether to just tell the truth or tell it the way she wanted it to be.

"No sir," Kate admitted. "I just wanted to beat the tar out of that boy."

Pa coughed. He had that twinkle in his eye and I could tell he wanted to laugh, but somehow he remained calm.

"Well Kate, it sounds like you did just that."

"Yes sir," said Kate softly, looking down at the floor.

"I'll talk with Clarence's father tomorrow. I want your word that neither of you will let this happen again. But I appreciate that the two of you have stood up for each other. Somehow I think you figured out something about love, even with an unorthodox approach."

That night as I worked on going to sleep, I thought about Pa's words and the events of the day. I didn't quite under-stand everything Pa had said, and I really didn't know if Kate had become an angel for a little while that day, but I was sure glad she was my sister.

# 12

# Unorthed Oxen Society

The following morning, Kate stayed unusually quiet as we did our chores. She had something on her mind. She didn't speak until we had walked halfway to school.

"Johnny," began Kate as we trudged along the path, "last night, Pa said we had an 'unorthed ox' approach. What's an unorthed ox?"

"I don't know, Kate. I've been thinking about that too. I don't know about the unorthed part. Maybe Pa's saying you're a little bull-headed sometimes."

"Oh, okay."

We walked a little farther.

"Johnny?"

"Yes, Kate?"

"Is it bad to be bull-headed?"

"I don't think so, Kate. Bull-headed means you stand up for what you believe in and you don't change your mind easily. I guess it means you're a bit stubborn, which probably helps you stick to your guns."

Kate pondered that a while.

"So, being stubborn is a good thing," said Kate. She thought a while longer. "Johnny?"

"Yes, Kate?"

"I think you're a bit stubborn too."

"Am I?"

"Yep, I think so. You might be like an unorthed ox too."

"So, Pa thinks you and I are a pair of unorthed oxen."

"Yep. Maybe we should form the Unorthed Oxen Society!" Kate exclaimed. "That could be our club! And anybody else who we think is bull-headed, we could invite them into the club too."

I smiled. "Kate, what would the Unorthed Oxen Society do?"

"Oh," she said, thinking for a moment. "Well, we would have meetings and talk about things we believe in. Or," she began, with a gleam in her eye, "we could talk about people who need to have some common sense beat into them." She laughed at that thought.

"You mean like Clarence?"

"Like Clarence."

I began laughing. "Pa won't really go for that, you know."

"I guess not. Maybe when we're older we can make our club. We'll need a secret code though."

"We could just speak and write in Hebrew. Not many people seem to know that."

"Well maybe, but I don't know yet how we're going to learn it."

We walked in silence the rest of the way to school, not because we had nothing to talk about, but because Kate was thinking so hard about Hebrew and her new club.

After supper that night, as Pa and Kate sat with Grandma by the fireplace, Kate decided to reveal her plans to Pa.

"Pa, would you call George, Elias, and Ott unorthed too?"

Pa looked at Kate with a blank stare.

Undaunted, Kate continued. "Are Johnny and I always unorthed, or does it just happen sometimes?"

"Kate, I'm not sure what you—" began Pa.

Kate interrupted Pa and said, "Last night you said something about how Johnny and I are like a pair of unorthed oxen. We decided to form the Unorthed Oxen Society, but I have to figure out if I can invite George, Elias, and Ott too. Are they also unorthed oxen?"

Pa's lips were pursed and his face turned red before he broke into one of his coughing fits. When he finally regained his composure, he asked, "Kate, that's a marvelous idea. May I join too?"

A few moments later, Grandma began chuckling, and soon she was cackling. In fact, she laughed so hard she had tears streaming down her cheeks. "Unorthed ... oxen," she gasped, before bursting into laughter again.

"Grandma, what's so funny?" asked Kate, obviously bewildered.

"Oh ... child, this is just something I will have to tell you when you get a bit older."

"Okay, Grandma," said Kate with a shrug, content with that answer. She picked up her doll and whispered, "Not everyone can be in the Unorthed Oxen Society, especially Clarence and that awful Eugene Dinwidden III."

# 13

# Eugene

With chubby cheeks and curly blond hair that made him look a whole lot nicer on the outside than he was on the inside, Eugene Dinwidden III had the rare ability to get under my skin, and he knew it. It all started with his name. I'm not sure if it was because his name sounded too city-like, or if maybe I was just jealous that he had a III behind his name and I didn't.

Eugene lived on the edge of town, within spittin' distance of the school. His father ran the local post office.

From the first day that I met Eugene it was clear that he didn't know anything about fishing, hunting, or even how to play a game of One Old Cat out in the schoolyard. It didn't bother me that he didn't know how to do those things. It bothered me that he didn't even want to learn, and then he would turn right around and criticize us for not playing with him. He usually wouldn't come outside when the rest of us were playing, saying how the cold air made him sickly ill, or the warm, humid air made him sickly ill, or too many mosquitoes might be bad for him, and so forth, and then he would whine and complain because the rest of us had fun and he didn't.

Even when we would agree to come inside and play with him, he would argue about the rules of whatever game we were playing; he would accuse us of cheating or of conspiring against him; and he would go into hysterics if he lost or excessive boasting if he won.

In short, Eugene Dinwidden III was a spoiled brat who couldn't be counted on for much of anything, including doing occasional chores around the schoolhouse and schoolyard.

On especially cold days, Miss Baines would send us boys out in pairs to get extra wood for the stove and to bring in snow that we could melt to get water. Often she would send Sam and me out as a team, until one day when Sam and I got a bit distracted by the excellent packing snow on the ground.

"I'm going to get you, Bobby Lee," shouted Sam.

"Not if I get you first, Ulysses S. Grant," I responded with a laugh. I'm not sure who threw the first snowball, but before we knew it the school yard had turned into a major snowball battlefield and we had an all-out war going.

Sam and I had so much fun that we quickly lost track of time and forgot all about going back inside. We must have been gone too long, and Miss Baines apparently decided to get our attention.

As I knelt on the ground, making a pile of snowballs in preparation for my next assault on Sam, a snowball hit me firmly in the back. Without thinking, I picked up a snowball and turned, firing it in the direction that the attacker's missile had come from. Miss Baines managed to duck out of the way, and the ball hit the person standing behind her, who happened to be Eugene Dinwidden III. It nailed him right smack in the forehead.

Miss Baines stood there at the door, shaking her head. I don't think the tears in her eyes were from feelings of remorse that Eugene had been hit by a snowball, but I'll never know that for sure.

Miss Baines gave me a mild scolding, and Kate later whispered to me that Pa would probably hear about this, either from Miss Baines or from Eugene's father, Eugene Dinwidden II.

That night, at supper, Pa said nothing about the incident. I knew better than to keep it silent, though. Pa much preferred to hear trouble from us than to hear trouble about us from somebody else.

"Pa?"

"Yes, Johnny."

"Pa, today when Miss Baines sent Sam and me out to get firewood, we were having a big snowball fight when—"

"Wait—let me get this straight. She sent you out to get firewood, and you were having a snowball fight?"

"Yes sir." I could tell that this wasn't going to go in the direction I was hoping.

"Johnny, why do you suppose you are going to school?"

"To get an education, sir, so that I can improve my lot in life."

"That's correct. And who wants you to try to do your very best in all things?"

"You do, sir."

"And?"

"Ma does too, sir."

"And?"

"And God does too."

"Good answer, Johnny. Now, don't you get play time during lunch, and don't you get play time after school?"

"Yes sir."

"I know that snowball fights are fun, and you and Sam are great friends. I like Sam. But sometimes when we're doing our chores—or gathering firewood for Miss Baines— we need to just get it done and get back to our other duties."

"Yes sir."

"Now, tell me the rest of the story."

"Well, I had used up all my snowballs, and I was making more for the next attack. A snowball hit me square in the back. I picked up a snowball from the ground and turned and threw it before I really looked to see where it was going."

"This doesn't sound good," sighed Pa.

"Well, the snowball headed right toward Miss Baines, who happened to be the one who threw the snowball at me."

Pa smiled. He and Ma had both liked Miss Baines and had a lot of say in getting her hired at the school.

"You hit Miss Baines?"

"No sir. She stepped out of the way, but the snowball hit the person standing behind her."

"Uh oh. I'm afraid to ask."

"Eugene Dinwidden III."

Pa started coughing. Try as he might, he failed in a brief struggle to hold back his laughter. I think I even detected a tear in his eyes.

"Is Eugene okay?" Pa choked.

"Yes sir, just a little bruised on his forehead."

"Well, that's not good, but I'm glad it's not worse than that. Johnny, be careful where you throw those snowballs. You've got a strong arm. I'd feel terrible if you had hit Miss Baines, or if Eugene had been badly hurt."

"Yes sir, I understand. I shouldn't have thrown it without looking."

"You shouldn't have thrown it while your task involved gathering firewood."

I nodded.

Later that evening, when everyone had gone to bed, I heard Pa break into laughter. In moments like that, he often spoke more loudly than he thought, and I heard him tell Ma, "Well, at least it might have knocked some sense into that Dinwidden boy."

# 14

# Gathering Firewood

"I need two volunteers to go out and bring in a load of firewood," said Miss Baines.

Two arms shot up in the air, one of them being mine and the other belonging to Sam. Miss Baines looked at us thoughtfully, and she smiled. "Johnny and Eugene, please go out and get some firewood for us."

I looked at Sam, whose arm had remained raised. His arm slowly came down.

I looked at Eugene, whose arm never had gone in the air. He did not look happy. The bruise on his forehead made him look even a bit mad.

"Miss Baines, I feel ill," said Eugene in a soft voice.

"Eugene, fresh air will do you some good," replied Miss Baines.

"Miss Baines, I'm afraid I might be getting the plague."

"The plague?"

"The plague. I hear it's going around in Des Moines, and it might be coming our way."

"Good heavens, we don't want the plague. I think then that you and Johnny should bring in twice the amount of firewood as usual, to make sure this schoolhouse doesn't get too cold. We certainly don't need the plague coming here."

"But, Miss Baines—"

"Eugene, do you want me to ask you to bring in three times the usual amount?"

"No ma'am."

"Then get going."

"Yes ma'am."

Eugene reluctantly put on his coat, hat, and mittens, and he followed me out the door.

Once outside, Eugene sat down on the schoolhouse steps.

"What are you doing, Eugene? We have to get the firewood."

"You can get it, can't you Johnny? Physical labor in the cold air doesn't agree with me."

"Doesn't agree with you?"

"Doesn't agree with me."

"What does agree with you, Eugene?"

"A cup of hot cocoa on a day like this would certainly agree with me."

I had to agree with that. "That does sound good," I admitted. "But listen, Eugene, sometimes chores just need to be done, and somebody's got to do them."

"Oh, I know that. But I don't need to be the one who does them. I'm going to grow up to have servants under me who do all this sort of stuff, so I don't need to learn it. That's what Mother and Father said."

"It's not about learning it, Eugene, it's about doing it. We don't have servants in the schoolhouse. All of us are students, and we have one teacher. She's busy teaching. Besides, she's the one who carries in the wood first thing in the morning, to get the fire started."

"Miss Baines brings in firewood?"

"Yes, Eugene, she does. And she melts the snow so that we'll have water. And she sweeps the floor, wipes the desks, cleans the slate board, and has the lessons prepared. Plus, don't forget, she has to help out with some of the chores where she's boarding."

Eugene thought about that a minute and then stood up.

"So, are you going to help?" I asked.

"No, of course not. But I'll watch you."

"Thanks Eugene," I muttered under my breath.

I walked to the nearby wood pile—Eugene followed at a distance that was close enough that I couldn't ignore him but far enough so that I wouldn't presume that he was willing to help—and began selecting pieces of wood to carry inside.

"What kind of wood is that?" Eugene asked.

"Mostly cottonwood, birch, elm, or oak."

"Where does it come from?"

"What do you mean where does it come from? It comes from trees."

"I know that, but who splits the wood and brings it here?"

"Pa and some of the other fathers do that," I said.

"How much does your Pa get paid for that?"

"Paid? He doesn't get paid for doing that."

"Why not?"

"Why should he?"

"Because it's work."

"Eugene, some things people just do because they need to get done, like chopping firewood to heat the schoolhouse."

"I wouldn't do it if I wasn't getting paid. That work is too hard to do for free."

The door to the schoolhouse opened. Eugene quickly picked up a piece of wood and put it in the bucket.

"Eugene, are you helping, or is Johnny doing all the work?"

"I'm doing most of the work, Miss Baines. Johnny's just talking. It's cold out though, so are we almost done?"

"I know it's cold, Eugene. That's why you are bringing in wood."

"Yes, Miss Baines."

She stepped back inside and closed the door. Eugene shrugged. "What else could I tell her?" he said. He walked back over to the steps and sat down.

I glared at Eugene. He had lied about me, right in front of me, and that bothered me considerably.

After we carried the wood back into the schoolhouse, Miss Baines came over to my desk and whispered, "Johnny, did Eugene do any work?"

I looked over at Eugene. He looked scared, and I knew he didn't want to get in trouble. I also didn't want to lie.

"Miss Baines," I said, "I think Eugene did about all that he has the ability to do."

Eugene looked relieved. Miss Baines thanked me and walked back to the front of the classroom.

After class, Eugene came up to me and told me, "Thanks for covering for me, Johnny."

"I didn't cover for you, Eugene. I told the truth."

"You told Miss Baines that I did all I'm capable of doing."

"Yes, and I believe that to be the honest truth. You did nothing, and that's about all you are capable of doing. You are a spoiled brat, Eugene."

"You take that back, Johnny Stevens."

"I will not," I retorted, and I walked away.

I thought about it more while walking home with Kate and Sam. What I had said to Eugene, I had said with a mean spirit. I could have been nicer, I know, but somebody had to tell Eugene, and if his parents neglected to tell him that he can't treat people so rudely, then I figured that I may as well do him the favor.

"What's eating at you, Johnny?" asked Kate, breaking the silence. "You're quieter than a dead church mouse."

"Oh, nothing. Just thinking about things," I replied. They didn't question me and allowed me to continue on in silence.

When we got home, I saw Elias out in the barn, repairing one of the animal troughs. "Can I help you, Elias?"

Elias looked at me and said, "Sure, Johnny. Tell you what. My fingers are numb from the cold, and I keep dropping the nails. Would you mind holding the nails while I get them started with the hammer?"

I didn't mind that a bit. Not that I didn't value my fingers, but I trusted the accuracy that Elias had with a hammer.

While he was pounding away, I talked to him. "Elias, lying is not a good thing. I know that."

"You got that right, brother," he agreed.

"Is it worse when someone says a lie about you right in front of you?"

"Well … that's a good question. A lie is a lie. But I guess if someone says a lie about you right in front of you, it makes you feel extra bad or something. Did someone tell a lie about you?"

He stopped hammering and looked at me.

"Yep," I admitted.

"Do you want me to help settle it?" In other words, did I want Elias to go and beat up whoever told the lie?

"No, Elias. It's okay, I guess. I just get so angry at Eugene."

When Elias finished up the hammering, he said I should help Ott. I found him out back in the fruit orchard, mending the fence to keep deer away from the apple trees.

"Ott, I know lying is wrong," I began.

Ott interrupted me. "Well, it depends. If you want to go to sleep, lying is a good thing. It's a lot harder to sleep when you're standing up. Now, if you're trying to walk into town, or you're playing a game of One Old Cat, then lying is a bad thing. But if you want to look at the clouds and see if you can find interesting shapes, it's easier lying than it is standing there with your neck bent trying to look upward."

Ott could be silly sometimes. He started laughing. "Does that help?"

I smiled. "No, not really. Well yeah, I guess it does actually. I was pretty mad, but now I'm not so mad."

He replied, "Well, you weren't pretty mad. When you were mad, you were kind of ugly. So I'd say maybe you were ugly mad." He chuckled at his own wit.

"Ott, you're silly today."

"Oh I know, Johnny. Just feeling in good humor."

After helping Ott with the fence, I went back inside the house and found Kate, sitting by the fireplace with Grandma, singing a song to her doll. Ma sat beside Kate, resting with her eyes closed. Ma had finished preparing dinner and the food remained on the stove, staying warm until the older boys came in from outside.

"Ma, what do you do when somebody lies about you?"

Ma reflected on that a moment. "I pray for that person, Johnny."

"You do? How come?"

"Johnny, when somebody says lies, it's usually because they're hurting on the inside for some reason. They need our prayers to help them get better. Does that make sense?"

"Yes, it does, Ma. But it's hard praying for somebody who lies about you."

"I know, Johnny. It is."

"I'll bet you are talking about Eugene Dinwidden III aren't you!" said Kate, emphatically, standing up and dropping her doll on the floor. "So that's what is bothering you. I'm going to go beat the living daylights out of that boy, and he'll regret he ever said anything to anybody about anything." She got worked up in a hurry.

Ma looked at Kate. "Kate, calm down. Eugene may have a mean streak, but we should let God administer any punishment."

"I know, but that takes the fun out of it, Ma. The least God could do is let us watch him beat Eugene up. I'd pay almost anything to see that." Then she giggled at that thought and went back to singing to her doll.

"Johnny," said Ma, "here is something I want you to think about. God asks us to forgive. Do you think he wants us to go around first, telling everybody how somebody wronged us, before we forgive that person?"

"I … I don't know, Ma."

"Give it some thought. I think you'll find the answer."

# 15

# Alexander Pierce

"Well, what do we have here?" asked Mr. Ledbetter, greeting us as Pa, Kate, and I walked into his store on a Saturday morning, the last day of March—in fact, the day before Easter. "Looks like the Stevens children have come to town and have brought their pa with them. How are you today, Miss Kate?" he said with a bow.

Kate smiled and did a curtsy in return. "I am fine, Mr. Ledbetter. How are you?"

"I am fine, Miss Kate. And what brings you here today?"

"We came to help Pa pick out an Easter hat for Ma," said Kate. "Ma wanted us to come with Pa because—"

"Kate," said Pa.

"Ma saw the hat that Mr. Landis bought for Mrs. Landis last year," continued Kate, "with artificial flowers, artificial fruit, and artificial birds, and—"

"Kate," repeated Pa.

"Ma said that the hat—"

"Kate," said Pa.

"—made Mrs. Landis look like a walking fruit garden," finished Kate. "Yes, Pa?"

Pa, who had turned beet red, said, "Never mind."

Mr. Ledbetter laughed. "Yes, I remember that hat," he said with a smile. Then he leaned over the counter and whispered, "You know something? Your Ma was right."

"Anyway, I know you have some beautiful hats here, and I'm sure we can find something that Ma will like," said Kate.

"Miss Kate, you are so polite and well-behaved—young Mr. Stevens, you are as well—and I think that is deserving of a candy stick from the jar, if it is okay with your pa."

All eyes turned to the candy jar on the counter, where we saw Mrs. Lincoln up on her hind legs, leaning against the jar and happily licking all of the candy sticks. She seemed especially fond of the purple colored sticks, probably raspberry flavored.

"Oh dear, someone left the lid off the jar again. They say that cats don't like sweets, but nobody told Mrs. Lincoln. She loves those candy sticks," sighed Mr. Ledbetter. "Well, so much for those. Guess I'll just have to throw them—"

Mr. Ledbetter found himself interrupted by a procession of kittens that marched around the corner and into the center aisle. In a moment, they were all prancing around our feet and singing a delightful chorus of high-pitched meows.

"They are so cute, Mr. Ledbetter," said Kate.

"Like them?" asked Mr. Ledbetter. "Go ahead, pick one up. In fact, I'm wondering if you could use some good mousers out at your place. John, what do you think?"

Pa stood there, holding an Easter hat that featured little wooden goldfish attached with wires, and when the hat moved, the goldfish appeared to be swimming. Kate looked at him and shook her head. Pa shrugged and set the hat back on the shelf.

"Mousers? As a matter of fact, we probably could use a couple. How much?"

"Oh, they'd be free to a good home like yours," said Mr. Ledbetter. "Pick out any two you want, but Mrs. Lincoln stays here," he said with a smile.

"All right then. Kate, pick one out; Johnny, you can pick the other," said Pa.

"Honest? Oh, Pa, thank you! Thank you, Mr. Ledbetter!" exclaimed Kate gleefully. "I kind of like this one," she said, referring to the orange and white kitten snuggled in her arms.

"And I like this one," I said, picking up a black and white kitten that had been gnawing at my shoes. "Thank you, Mr. Ledbetter."

"If I'm not mistaken, this orange one is a girl … and the black and white one is a boy," said Mr. Ledbetter. He quickly confirmed what he had said. "Now the hard part—what are you going to name them?"

"I think I'm going to name mine Grandpa Shideler," I said with a smile. "I'll share him with Grandma, and he can help keep her company."

"I think she'll like that, Johnny," agreed Pa. "Kate, how about you?"

"I think I'll name her Easter."

"That name sounds about as perfect as can be," said Pa, smiling.

Mr. Ledbetter's smile became serious. "Say John, have you seen any black bears down on your property?"

"Black bears? No sir, can't say that I have," said Pa.

"Apparently Lucas Hahn saw one the other day—a large male—trying to attack his pigs. Lucas shot the bear, but where there's one, there could always be more."

"I'll keep my eyes open. Thanks for the warning."

The door to Ledbetter's opened and in walked Mr. Kilpatrick with his top hat, cane, and sinister smile.

Mrs. Lincoln hissed, and she and the rest of her kittens quickly vanished somewhere in the back of the store.

"Stevens, Ledbetter," he said. "It's a glorious day, isn't it?"

"Yes, it is, Horace. Easter season is always glorious," said Pa.

I knew that wasn't what Mr. Kilpatrick meant, and Pa knew it too.

"Posh, Easter," snorted Mr. Kilpatrick. "Is it Easter already? When, tomorrow? Well, Easter will have to go on without me. I have far too much to do. Tomorrow I'll be planning my next steps with the Pierce property."

"Alexander Pierce?" asked Pa.

"Alexander Pierce, yes indeed," said Mr. Kilpatrick. "It seems Pierce is going to miss his monthly payment. The payment is due Tuesday, and if he doesn't pay it, the inn that he runs—the Polk City Inn—is mine, all mine.

"He's losing the inn?"

"For all practical purposes, he has already lost the inn,'" said Mr. Kilpatrick. "Yes sir, come Tuesday, there will be a new sign out front: Polk City Inn, Horace Kilpatrick, Proprietor. Oh my, what a glorious day." Mr. Kilpatrick licked his lips before smiling widely.

"But that inn is how he makes his living. If he doesn't have that inn, he'll have nothing," said Pa, softly but firmly.

"Well, then Pierce should have done a better job managing his money, eh? Besides, I think Pierce is too soft. He does not require nearly enough money from the patrons who stay at his inn, and it costs him dearly. It will cost him everything."

Mr. Kilpatrick said that last sentence the same way a judge might tell an outlaw that he had been sentenced to be hanged under the big oak tree at high noon the next day. For a moment, the world stood still. It wasn't what he said that had bothered me. It was how he said it. If Mr. Kilpatrick were a child—one of Pa's children—Pa would have taken him behind the wood shed and given him a lesson in what a birch stick feels like on the back side. I don't think Mr. Kilpatrick had ever experienced that.

"Yes, it's a glorious day," said Mr. Kilpatrick. "Now let's see … what did I … oh yes. Ledbetter, I would like a handful of your candy sticks please. An assortment of flavors would be nice."

Mr. Ledbetter reached out and grabbed all the sticks in the open jar on the counter, and he placed them in a bag for Mr. Kilpatrick. Mr. Ledbetter gave me a slight, almost imperceptible wink. "Here you go, Mr. Kilpatrick. I hope you enjoy them. These are the cat's meow, as they say."

Mr. Kilpatrick pulled out a raspberry candy stick from the bag. He looked at it for a moment, and then he put it in his mouth. "Delicious, Ledbetter. Glorious, simply glorious."

Mr. Kilpatrick headed for the door. "Ledbetter, Stevens, enjoy the day. I know I will."

As he pulled open the door, Kate said, "Good day, Mr. Kilpatrick." He turned and looked at her a moment, and at first I thought he might say something. Then he simply turned and left, allowing the door to slam shut behind him.

On the way home, we rode in silence a while. Kate and I were playing with the kittens in the back of the wagon. Finally I asked, "Pa, what is Mr. Pierce going to do?"

Pa didn't answer right away. He sat there, scratching his chin.

"I don't know, son. I don't quite know."

"Sounds like he's in a bind, Pa."

"Yes, it does, Johnny."

We rode the rest of the way home. Pa wasn't saying much of anything, but he seemed to me to be in deep thought.

As we pulled into the farm, Pa said, "Johnny, Kate, something is tugging at my heart. I've got an idea and am thinking about going back into town to see some folks. The trip may take a couple of hours. Besides, I was so distracted at Ledbetter's that I forgot to buy the Easter hat for Ma." Pa chuckled.

"Pa," said Kate, "may I stay here and play with our new kittens?"

"Sure, Kate," said Pa. "Johnny, want to come along?"

"Yes sir."

Pa stepped into the house, and I heard him say something to Ma. He walked out a minute or two later and climbed on the wagon.

"Let's go!" he said.

What happened after that might have gone down in Iowa history as the Polk City Miracle—that is, if anybody had found out about it.

# 16

# Polk City Miracle

We rode first to Ledbetter's General Store, where Pa purchased a nice blue Easter hat for Ma, and then we rode on to Alexander Pierce's Polk City Inn. Mrs. Pierce stood on the front porch, sweeping.

"Good morning, Mrs. Pierce. Is Alexander home?"

"Morning, Mr. Stevens. Yes, he is. Let me go get him." She stepped off the porch and walked around behind the inn. A moment later, Alexander appeared, wiping his hands on a cloth rag. I noticed that Mr. Pierce looked tired, worn out, almost as if he had been in a fight and had decided that he probably ought to give up. His wife looked about the same, with the worry lines furrowed deep into her forehead.

"John, what can I do for you?" said Mr. Pierce, softly.

"Alexander, it's not my place to pry, but I ran into Horace Kilpatrick at Ledbetter's and I heard some unsettling news. I'm wondering if there's anything I can do to help."

"Not unless you happen to have two hundred dollars magically appear at your feet, there's not," he said.

"So what's going to happen?" asked Pa.

"Mrs. Pierce and I will probably head back east. It's a shame, though. Things at the inn were going so well. That is, until Mr. Kilpatrick took over at the bank."

"Why do you say that?" asked Pa.

"Why? I'll tell you why. Simply put, one of my deposits that I made with the bank never got recorded. They say they have no record of it."

"It's lost?"

"It's lost. I know I took it to the bank though. Mrs. Pierce accompanied me, in fact. But Horace says I didn't pay it."

"Do you have a receipt for the payment?" asked Pa.

"No, I can't find it. I did have it—I'm sure I put it where I put all the other receipts—but it's not there. I don't know where it could have gone."

"We've searched the inn thoroughly," said Mrs. Pierce, "but there's no receipt for last month. Alexander has always been so careful with the bank receipts, too."

Pa and Mr. Pierce talked a bit longer, and then Pa came back to the wagon. We drove off in silence, but instead of heading toward home, we continued the opposite way.

Pa stopped at Adam Thornton's home. Mr. Thornton, the local potter, went to the same church we did.

"Stay here, Johnny. I'll just be a few minutes."

Pa walked up to the door and knocked, and someone let him in. True to his word, ten minutes later Pa returned.

"Why'd we stop here, Pa?" I asked. Pa didn't reply.

That morning, we stopped at another eight or nine homes in town—all people Pa knew well—and Pa went into the homes to talk while I stayed out with the wagon. We visited John Schaal, Doc Hubbard, and a few others. I didn't know exactly what Pa had in mind, but eventually it dawned on me. Pa wanted to collect money from the people we visited so that the community could help out the Pierce family, and Pa did not want me to know who contributed and who didn't. Pa kept a serious face throughout the morning as we went from house to house, but on the way to our last stop—back at the Pierce's home—he broke into a smile.

"I didn't know for sure how this would play out, but I do know this. God is good. He is certainly good."

I didn't say anything. I didn't have to. I knew I would remember this moment as long as I lived.

Charlie, the Pierce's dog, came out to greet us as we pulled to a stop in front of the inn shortly after noon. Mr. and Mrs. Pierce both stepped out onto the porch of their inn and were looking at us with curiosity.

"Hello, John," said Mr. Pierce, still on the porch. "What brings you back here?"

Pa didn't say anything as he stepped down from the wagon, but he had a smile on his face that he couldn't hide.

"Alexander, Mrs. Pierce, I have the privilege of presenting ... well, just remember that this isn't from me. I'm only the messenger. This is something that God himself made happen."

Mr. Pierce had a puzzled look on his face. "I'm not sure what you mean, John," he stammered, "and I'm almost afraid to ask."

"Well, I felt led to wander around and ask folks—anyone who might feel willing to help you out a bit—to contribute. I'm not going to give you any names and I won't tell you who contributed how much, but in this envelope right here"—Pa pulled an envelope from his coat pocket—"we have a total sum of $245."

Mr. Pierce gasped, and Mrs. Pierce's hands went to her face immediately to hide her tears.

"John, how can we ever repay you ... how can we ever repay everybody who—"

"Alexander," Pa interrupted, "first of all, there is no repayment to be made. This is a gift. Folks who know you and love you contributed this out of their own generosity. Just accept it, use it to pay off your debt, and do what you feel is best with the excess."

They shook hands, and then Pa and I rode in silence back home. Pa didn't have to say anything. His smile said it all.

When we were almost within sight of the house, a question came to mind. "Pa, how did you know you'd be able to get the money?"

"Johnny, I don't want to talk about it too much. Not that it's wrong, but I don't want to find myself feeling too prideful over helping someone out. We shouldn't think too much about where we have been, only about where we're going."

I could understand that.

I wish I could have seen the look on Mr. Kilpatrick's face when Alexander Pierce gave him the money that following Monday. Pa did go with Mr. Pierce to the bank—Pa went as a witness in case anyone ever doubted whether Mr. Pierce paid up—but Pa wouldn't let me go with him.

After I went to bed that night, I overhead Pa telling Ma that Mr. Kilpatrick had a fit when Pa and Mr. Pierce walked into the bank with the money. "He acted like a two-year-old whose candy stick was taken away between licks," said Pa.

"Some people just don't quite grow up, do they," said Ma.

"Maybe," said Pa, "or maybe it's that some people grow up too much and they forget to enjoy the simple things of life."

# 17

# Black Bear Bridge

"Well how about that?" said George. "So far, it looks like we won't be eating much for dinner. Let's go check the other one."

Talking and laughing on an early May morning near the end of the planting break from school, we plodded through the mud on our way toward the second trap. Even from a distance, we could tell that the trap had caught something. George broke into a run toward the trap, and I followed right behind. We found the torn, shredded remains of a rabbit. Fur and blood mixed in with the surrounding mud.

"Do you think a wolf or coyote got it, George?"

"Look at these tracks," he said, pointing a few feet away. "What do you think?"

In the mud lay a large paw print that dwarfed any animal track I had ever seen. "Bear?"

George nodded. "I think so. Let's get home."

We walked home briskly, frequently glancing over our shoulders. We saw no sign of a bear.

Pa went back out in the woods with us to look at the paw print, and he confirmed that it was a bear track.

"Be on your toes," he warned. "These are fresh tracks. This isn't the same bear that Mr. Hahn shot before Easter."

Later that morning, I worked in the garden, weeding and planting seeds with Ma and Kate. Ma was telling funny stories about when she was little. She had me laughing so hard that I all but forgot about the bear.

When we were just about done planting seeds, Sam appeared around the corner of the house. "Hello, Mrs. Stevens. Hi Johnny, Kate."

"Hello, Sam," said Ma.

"Mrs. Stevens, can Johnny come fishing?" Sam asked.

I looked at Ma, who nodded. "Just remember, boys," she said, "that the bridge railing is rotting and Pa doesn't want you putting your weight against it."

"Thank you, Ma!" I shouted, and within minutes Sam and I were walking briskly toward the creek. Down on the banks of the creek, the moist, rich, fertile earth teemed with fishing worms, and soon we had our sticks and lines in the water as we sat on the bridge, waiting for that first bite to come.

The warmth of the early afternoon sun seemed to bring the fish to life, and within a few minutes we had caught a medium sized catfish and a small pan fish.

Stretching my arms, I leaned my head back and let the sun's rays cover my face. "Fishing—I could do this all day long, every day of the year. I'm not ready for the planting break to end, but Ma and Pa say schooling is important."

"Yep, mine too. It's tough sittin' in the classroom all day long though, Johnny."

"Sam, what do you want to be when you grow up?"

Sam paused a moment, seeming to be in thought. Then he smiled and said, "I know exactly what I want to be, or rather, who I want to be. I want to be you."

"Me?"

"Yep, you."

"Why?"

"Well, 'cause I figure that you might want to be me, and if you are me then I can't be me too—there's only room for one of us in me." Sam smiled.

"Furthermore," he continued, "if I'm you and you are me, then I'll end up being me. And where will you be? Nowhere to be found!"

"Sam Hudson, you have strange ideas," I laughed. "I meant what do you want to be, not who do you want to be."

"I don't know, Johnny. My pa farms. His pa farmed. And my pa's grandfather farmed."

"I recognize a pattern there."

"You're pretty bright, Johnny Stevens."

"Takes a bright one to know a bright one."

"Johnny, what do you want to be?"

"I don't know, Sam. I love the farm, but sometimes it seems like there's something else I need to be doing. Right now I need more adventure in my life or something."

"Such as?"

"I don't know. Maybe I could be a lawyer. It seems like big people need help in remembering how they are supposed to treat each other."

"A lawyer! You know what my dad says about lawyers?"

"I'm afraid to ask."

"Do you know the difference between a lawyer and a rattlesnake?"

"I give up."

"The rattlesnake has the courtesy to let you know before it strikes."

"Ouch. Okay, maybe I want to be a preacher."

"A preacher? Yes, I can see you doing that. Problem is, Johnny, that when you go and talk to folks about how they should live and how they should keep faith even during hard times, they'll ask you about your problems and how you managed them."

"So?"

"So, you haven't had any trials, Johnny Stevens. You haven't had suffering or a lot of hurt or things like that."

"Like I said before: So?"

"You've got to prove your mettle."

"Sam, how old are we?"

"Ten, Johnny, but sometimes it feels like thirty."

"You sound old. Thirty! That's about as old as the hills."

"Hi Johnny! Hi Sam!" said Kate as she stepped onto the bridge. Sam and I stood up.

"Hello, Miss Kate, and welcome to our kingdom," replied Sam. Sam bowed and I followed suit, and then I leaned against the railing.

"Johnny," exclaimed Kate. "Don't touch—"

But it was too late. With a splintering CRACK!, the wooden rail broke and I fell into the creek with a big splash!

"Johnny! Johnny, are you okay?" Sam cried out.

"A little wet, I suppose," I grimaced, "but I'm okay."

"How's the water, Johnny?" asked Kate.

"It's frigid! Here, try some," I said, taking my hand and splashing it in the creek, spraying Kate with cold water.

I made my way over to the side of the creek, climbed out, and stood up on shore next to the small stand of trees and bushes that separated the creek from our fields. It felt good to be in the warm air, and I intended to drip off for a few minutes.

Moments after I climbed out, however, I heard movement in the bushes behind me. A baby black bear poked his head out of the bushes, startling me.

"Sam, Kate, look at this! It's a bear cub!"

"Oh, he's so cute!" said Kate.

"Johnny, if there's a cub, the mama is around here somewhere," said Sam.

"You're right, Sam. We should get out of here."

My words came too late. No sooner had I finished saying those words than I heard a crash of branches, and the mother bear appeared out of the bushes. She growled and didn't look too happy with me right next to her cub. She started thundering toward me!

I began to run, but I knew I couldn't outrun the bear. I also didn't want to go back out on the bridge, where the bear might come after Kate and Sam too.

"Help!" I screamed, as I ran up from the creek bed toward the house. The bear was gaining on me. I could hear her pounding on the earth right behind me. As I ran, I realized I had no chance of making it across the field.

Bang! A blast from a shotgun rang out.

I glanced behind me. The bear had stopped and was just standing there with a confused look on her face. I glanced in the direction of the gun shot. Elias was running full-speed toward the bear, holding his rifle and yelling. Right behind Elias was Ott, shouting and running toward the bear.

Elias stopped, quickly reloaded the shotgun, and fired another shot in the air. The bear took one quick look at me, looked back at Elias and Ott, and then she lumbered across the field and into the woods.

"You missed her, Elias!" said Ott, gasping for breath when he reached us.

"I wasn't trying to hit her, just scare her," said Elias. "I don't think this shotgun is going to kill any bear, and I didn't want to wound her without killing her, or she might end up madder than all get out."

"Thanks, brother," I said to Elias.

Elias didn't say anything at first. He set the gun down and gave me a big hug. It seemed to me for a while that he had no plans of ever letting go.

Finally he spoke. "I'm not the one to thank. Some voice in the back of my mind told me to get the shotgun out this morning and do some hunting. I had planned on heading down to the creek when I saw you running back up. I'm just glad that I listened to that voice."

"Funny how God does that sometimes," said Ott.

"Johnny, you okay?" came the breathless gasp of Sam Hudson, who, with Kate, had run up behind me.

"Yes, Sam, thanks to Elias."

"Hey," began Kate, "I thought of a name for the bridge. We should call it Black Bear Bridge."

Elias nodded. "Black Bear Bridge sounds good to me."

"Then Black Bear Bridge it is!" I shouted.

It wasn't until later that evening that the fright of being chased by a bear really sank in. I decided that the break from school had been adventurous enough and I found myself ready to spend some time in the classroom again.

# 18

# Sweltering

"You awake, Ott?" I asked. I figured I knew the answer already. It's funny how you can know that the person sleeping next to you is awake or asleep, whether you hear something or not.

"Yep. I'm enjoying sweating too much to be able to fall asleep," he answered.

"It's fun, ain't it?" I sighed.

"It would be more fun if we could have a night like this once in a while in the winter and have a cold winter night once in a while in the summer."

"I like that idea, Ott."

"Don't you think your body would break into pieces like glass, changing from zero degrees to a hundred degrees in only a day?" said Elias, piping in from across the room.

"You awake, too, Elias?" I asked.

"No, he's talking in his sleep," laughed George. "Wait a moment and you'll hear him pining for that pretty Abby Hubbard. 'Oh, Abby, Abby, will you dance with me, sweet Abby?'"

I heard a muffled thump—obviously Elias' pillow coming down on George's face—followed by laughter from both George and Elias.

"Abby Hubbard, really," said Ott. "Elias has no more chance of dancing with Abby at tomorrow's Fourth of July celebration than we have of finding snow on the ground in the morning."

I heard a muffled thump again, this time much closer, as a pillow—Elias' again—struck the wall behind our bed, right between Ott and me.

"Boys!" Pa's voice called out from his room. "Get some sleep, or the only dancing you'll be doing tomorrow is up and down the cornrows hoeing weeds while the rest of us are enjoying the festivities."

"Yes, Pa," said George.

"Yes, Pa," said Elias.

"Yes, Pa," said Ott.

"Yes, Pa," I said.

I heard Kate's voice come from the other room, but I couldn't quite make out what she was saying. Whatever it was, it set Grandma to cackling, which in turn got both Ma and Pa laughing.

"Adults!" shouted Ott. "Get some sleep, or you'll be joining us hoeing the cornrows."

"Yes, Ott," said Pa.

"Yes, Ott," said Ma.

"Yes, Ott," cackled Grandma.

After some silence, Ott shouted, "Kate, that means you too."

"Yes, Ott," laughed Kate.

A few minutes later, I was still awake. The heat was almost suffocating, and every bit of movement made me sweat.

"Ott? You still awake?" I whispered, not wanting to cross Pa.

"Yep," Ott replied.

"Why does God make it so hot on one end of the year and so cold on the other end? Couldn't he kind of average the days and make them just right?"

"I don't know, Johnny. Maybe he's already doing a lot to make our lives nicer."

"What do you mean?"

"Maybe, without God, the hot days would be hotter and the cold days would be colder. No, that can't be it. Without God, there wouldn't be days and nights. Without God, there wouldn't be life."

"So why does he make the days this way?"

"I don't know. Maybe if he makes it too nice down here, we won't want to get to heaven. Maybe that's why things aren't always easy. If we get too complacent, we won't see that we really need him."

"Ott?" said Elias.

"What, Elias?" asked Ott.

"For being my little brother, you seem wise sometimes."

"Let's get some sleep," said George.

Not another word was said until morning.

# 19

# Fourth of July

The morning of the Fourth of July, a bustle of activity in the kitchen woke us up earlier than usual. I walked into the kitchen to see what was causing the commotion, and I found Ma putting the finishing touches on the top crusts of two pies.

"You're up early, Ma. Are we having this for breakfast?"

Ma laughed. "No, Johnny. I know you love my pies, but this is for the pie contest at today's festivities."

"What kind of pies are they, Ma?"

"You'll have to wait and see, Johnny. One is for the contest and the other is for us to eat."

I tried to guess by looking around for fruit scraps, but Ma had already cleaned up. A couple of jars of peaches sat on the table, though, so I figured Ma might have made peach pies.

After we finished chores and had breakfast, we loaded up the wagon. Grandma and Kate packed the picnic basket for our lunch; George, Elias, and Ott brought their guns for the shooting contest; and I brought my bat and ball, hoping to get a game of One Old Cat going. Ma brought the blankets to sit on and a basket with the two pies. Pa, the last to get on the wagon, carried his large canvas backpack with him. Pa said, "Giddup!" and we headed on into Polk City for the Fourth of July Festival.

"Johnny! Johnny, over here!" I heard a familiar voice yell as Pa brought the wagon to a stop near the town square. I saw Sam, standing there with his parents and his sister.

"We hope you will join us, Catherine," said Mrs. Hudson to Ma, who smiled and laid the blankets on the ground next to the Hudson's blanket, thus staking out our territory.

"The parade starts in about thirty minutes, John," said Mr. Hudson, who also had a canvas backpack. "We're supposed to meet over behind the Town Hall." Pa didn't say anything, but he picked up his backpack, and he and Mr. Hudson headed across to the Town Hall building on the southern edge of the square.

"Come on Johnny," said Sam, "let's move to the front so we can see better." Sam and I went and found a shady spot along the edge of the parade route.

"Johnny! Sam!" a voice called out. I recognized it immediately as belonging to Eugene Dinwidden III. "Hi Johnny, hi Sam," he exclaimed when he reached us. "Are you having fun so far?"

"Yes, I suppose so," I responded cautiously. Eugene wasn't acting his usual self. It wasn't like him to be friendly to anybody.

"So, are you going to sign up for any of the contests?" he asked. "Did your mothers enter the pie contest?"

"Yes, Ma made a pie," I said.

"Mine too," said Sam.

"Oh, I bet they will be wonderful," Eugene said. "What kind of pie did your ma bake, Johnny?"

"Actually, I'm not sure, but it might be a peach pie."

"A peach pie? Oh I love peach pies. I am sure it will be delicious," Eugene said. He fidgeted with a small pouch hanging around his neck.

"What's in your pouch, Eugene?" I asked, curious.

Eugene's face turned beet red. "I ... I think my mother is calling for me. I'll talk to you later." He then ran off across the square.

"That boy is up to something, Johnny, I guarantee it," said Sam.

"He sure is, but I don't know what," I said. We both continued watching Eugene. He headed for the pie table.

A man dressed in a white suit, Mayor Hickman, stepped onto the platform and held his arms up in the air, commanding silence. He said a prayer, and then he gave the signal to fire a cannon, starting the parade. All eyes—except mine and Sam's—were on the parade. Eugene stood at the pie table, but he had his back to us and we really couldn't see what he was doing. Sam and I turned to glance at the parade, and in moments we had forgotten all about Eugene.

At the front of the parade came a flag bearer, proudly carrying the United States flag on a pole. He walked with dignity, and all of us clapped as he walked past us. Next came the soldiers who had fought in the rebellion. Some were missing arms, and some were missing legs. A horse-pulled wagon carried the men who couldn't walk. Pa and Mr. Hudson, dressed in their uniforms, walked next to each other behind the wagon. Not a sound could be heard as these soldiers approached. We heard only their solemn, somber footsteps—tramp, tramp, tramp—and as the soldiers marched along the street, their haggard faces shrouded with both pride and sadness, I felt a shiver go up my spine, a sense of gratitude for these men who had risked their lives in service to their country. I wanted to clap or shout, but I didn't know the proper thing to do. Tramp, tramp, tramp, the soldiers continued marching.

Finally one man in the crowd started clapping. Moments later, another joined in. Then, all at once, applause erupted. Shouts of "hurray!" and "thank you!" filled the air. Some of the soldiers had tears in their eyes, as did some of the people in the crowd. These were the war heroes, the men who performed in real life what Sam and I enjoyed acting out.

After the parade, the games and contests began. George, Elias, Ott, Kate, and I, along with Sam and his sister, entered a big tug-of-war game. Hatchet-throwing, horseshoes, log-splitting, wrestling, and other field games rounded out most of the morning. Elias won the shooting contest, held in Mr. Olofson's field a couple of blocks north of the square, and for his victory he was given a silver dollar.

For lunch we sat on our blanket next to the Hudsons, and our two families shared food. Grandma had made a delicious potato salad and fried chicken, and the Hudsons brought two loaves of wheat bread, a basket full of homemade sausages, and fresh cheese. We had a feast.

Grandma stood up and said, "I'll be right back."

"Can I come with you, Grandma?" asked Kate.

"No child, I have something I need to do," said Grandma, who gave us a wink before walking away. We watched her as she approached the stage and talked with Mayor Hickman.

"What's Grandma doing?" I asked.

"I don't know for sure," said Pa, "but I suspect she is up to something."

"Ma, the judges are looking at the pies now," said Kate excitedly. We were sitting quite a ways from the pie table, so we couldn't really see the judges responses.

"I know," said Ma, trying not to show her nervousness. She took pride in her pies and, though she didn't expect to win, she wanted to represent the family well.

"I think all the ribbons are out," said Kate. "Should I go see if you won?"

"No, dear," replied Ma. "If my rhubarb pie won, some-one will come tell me." My heart leaped when I heard those words. Ma's rhubarb pies were my favorite.

At that moment, the mayor stepped onto the stage and said, "Ladies and gentlemen, we have a special announce-ment. The first-place ribbon for this year's pie contest goes to Mrs. Hudson for her blueberry pie; in second place is Mrs. Stevens with her rhubarb pie; and Mrs. Ledbetter comes in at third with her cherry pie."

Everyone applauded, and Ma looked relieved. "I'm so happy for you, Mary," said Ma. Pa squeezed Ma's hand and smiled at her.

"Ma, can we have some of your pie now?" I asked.

"Let's wait until we've all finished our meals," said Ma.

"Sam, let's go look at the ribbons," I said, standing up. "Race you, Johnny!"

Sam hopped up and we raced to the pie table. Expect-ing to find a celebration for the winner, instead we found commotion, with Mrs. Dinwidden arguing with the judges. Eugene Dinwidden III stood behind her. Three ribbons—a blue, a red, and a white—lay on the table in front of the winning pies.

"Surely you must know a finely cooked pie when you see it," said Mrs. Dinwidden, holding a peach pie with a latticed top. I had to admit that the pie looked beautiful. "I made this pie with the finest of peaches. How could a com-mon blueberry pie or a rhubarb pie—ugh, that is a ghastly thought—finish higher than a delicate peach pie? I used the finest of spices, imported from Europe. I used an ex-pensive peach liqueur for flavoring. This recipe has never lost a pie contest!" shouted Mrs. Dinwidden, making a fool of herself with her tantrum. I thought back to Ma's reaction at not winning, and I felt glad and grateful that I had the ma I had.

"Mrs. Dinwidden, did you actually taste your pie?" asked one of the judges.

"Well, no, I didn't, but I have made this pie dozens of times and I know exactly how it tastes."

"I invite you to try a bite of your own pie, Mrs. Dinwidden," said the man, apparently the head judge, as he handed Mrs. Dinwidden a fork with a bit of her pie on it. Mrs. Dinwidden put the fork in her mouth and her face shriveled up in a horrible expression.

She began coughing and choking, and she gasped, "Salt! Someone has poured salt on my pie! Water, please, bring me some water."

Eugene's face quickly paled. He quickly put his hand over the little pouch on the string around his neck. I glared at Eugene a moment, but he wouldn't look me in the eye. Sam and I thought it best to leave the table. That was the last we saw of the Dinwiddens that day.

When we returned to the blankets, we found Grandma looking more nervous than a mouse in a barn full of cats. I didn't know why. I knew better than to ask, though, and I figured I would just have to wait to see what she had up her sleeve. I didn't have to wait long.

"And now it's time for the pig callin' contest," announced Mayor Hickman from the stage. "Would all contestants please come to the stage?"

"Let's go listen to the hog callin'," said Grandma, grabbing me by the hand and leading the way. We watched as each contestant took a turn up on the stage and spent one minute trying to impress the judges. Most calls sounded like loud squeals or variations on "Suey!" We laughed pretty hard through most of it.

The announcer took the stage and said, "We have one more entrant, a very special person whom I am positive you will enjoy. Mrs. Shideler, the stage is yours."

Grandma stepped onto the stage! A hush fell upon the audience like a blanket. I looked back where we had been sitting, and I saw Ma, Pa, and the others all running toward the stage to watch. Grandma smiled and then she began.

First, she crouched and leaned forward, making a clicking noise on the back of her tongue. She got into a rhythm, and then she started softly singing:

> *Pig-a-pig-a-pig-a-pig-GEE,*
> *pig-a-pig-a-pig.*
> *Pig-a-pig-a-pig-a-pig-GEE,*
> *pig-a-pig-a-pig.*

Grandma followed this with loud shouts of, "Pig! Pig!" and "Suey! Suey!" All the while, she pranced and danced on stage, clearly enjoying having an audience. The crowd smiled but remained respectfully silent.

"Suey! Suey!" she shouted, and then she went on a tear.

> *Pig-a-pig-a-pig-a-pig-GEE,*
> *pig-a-pig-a-pig.*
> *Suey! Suey! Suey! Suey!*
> *Pig-a-piggy!*
> *Suey! Suey!*
> *Pig-a-pig-a-pig-GEE-pig-GEE-piggity-pig!*
> *Suuuuuuuuu-eeeeeeeey!*

The crowd burst into laughter as this woman in her eighties danced around on stage, calling the pigs. When she finished, the audience gave her a standing ovation. With sweat rolling down her cheeks and out of breath, Grandma took a curtsy and stepped down from the stage.

"Grandma, I didn't know you could do that!" exclaimed Kate, and we all agreed.

Grandma smiled and said, "I won the hog callin' three years in a row as a little girl, and I figured I wanted to give it one more shot."

Moments later, the main judge stepped back onto the stage. "Is there any doubt as to this year's winner? Mrs. Shideler, you have won first place."

Grandma blushed, suddenly a bit embarrassed at her silly antics, but she stepped onto the stage and accepted her ribbon, which she carried proudly the rest of the afternoon.

Sam, Ott, and I all tried the next event, a pie-eating contest. They gave me an apple pie with a crust on top. By the time the contest finished, apple pie covered my entire face and nearly stuffed my nose. I didn't win, but for the rest of the day everything smelled like apple pie to me, and I didn't mind that for one moment.

The festivities ended with a square dance. Sam and I weren't particularly partial to dancin', so we sat on the hay bales and watched. The grown-ups seemed to enjoy it though.

We rode home before nightfall, quickly did the evening chores, and then we children crawled into bed, thoroughly exhausted. Even though it was just as hot as the night before, I fell asleep almost as soon as my head hit the pillow. Visions of soldiers marching, foot races, and apple pies were in my dreams all night long. When I awoke the next morning, everything still smelled like apple pie.

# 20

# Mama's Boy

As the summer went on, the heat continued its relentless pounding, day after day. The back half of July was as hot as the front half, and by mid-August we still had not seen enough rain to wet a whistle since the torrential downpours of March. Instead of reaching up to the deep blue Iowa sky as it usually did, the corn was beginning to shrivel.

The heat and drought seemed to make everybody just a little more irritable, me included, and the last thing I needed on that Friday morning as I walked to school myself—Kate had a mild fever and stayed home—was an encounter with Clarence Slaughter. Sure enough, as I turned the corner about halfway to school, there he was.

"Well, well, well, if it ain't Johnny Stevens. You are later than usual, and I was beginning to get worried that I wouldn't get to see my little buddy."

"I, uh, I had some chores to finish for Ma," I stammered.

"Chores? I should have figured you do chores. I'll bet you are a regular mama's boy," said Clarence Slaughter in about as mean-spirited a way as an eleven-year-old boy could say anything. I didn't respond. I just kept walking.

"Ain't that right?" Clarence called out.

I tried to ignore him.

"Johnny, ain't that right?" asked Clarence, as I unsuccessfully tried to maneuver around him without being noticed.

"I'm not a mama's boy, Clarence," I retorted.

"Are too."

"Am not. And how would you know? You've never been to my place."

"Well, I just know because you act like one."

"How does a mama's boy act?"

"Like a sissy. I'll bet anything that you're always helping out, doing chores and all."

I didn't really understand what the problem with helping Ma out with chores was; Ma and Pa had taught us that we're supposed to do those things.

"Clarence, what do you do if you don't do any chores around your house?"

"What do I do? Why Johnny, I do anything that I please. Nobody tells me what to do. Oh, what a life. I'm the king of my own kingdom. I can just sit back and look for opportunities to make some money come my way, like this here."

He pulled a leather pouch out of his pocket. "Know what's in here? It's ten dollars, all for me. Know how I got it? Well, I ain't gonna tell you, least ways not yet."

Something about this just didn't feel right, but I didn't feel like crossing Clarence Slaughter at the moment.

"Johnny, I'm forming the Anti Mama's Boy Club beginning right now, and you can sign on as a charter member. Are you in? Because if you ain't in, I'm going to have to beat you to a pulp."

I didn't feel courageous enough to say no to Clarence. All kinds of things were going through my mind at that moment, but I really wasn't keen on getting beaten to a pulp. "I guess I'm in, Clarence."

"Johnny, you tell your ma tonight that you ain't doing chores. Report back to me on Monday."

"All right, Clarence." I felt disappointed in myself for not standing up to Clarence, but I wasn't too excited about the possibility of encountering his fists.

The afternoon passed too quickly, probably because I didn't want to have to go home and begin the rebellion. The century had already faced one great rebellion, and I figured a second rebellion might be too much for Ma and Pa to handle. Besides worrying about incurring the wrath of one or both of my parents, it just didn't feel like it was the thing I should be doing. In church I had learned to honor my father and mother, and I knew deep in my heart that was the right thing to do. I went ahead and planned my rebellion though.

"Johnny, I need an onion cut up," said Ma, shortly after I got home.

"Ma, I can't."

"You can't?"

"I mean I won't."

"Johnny Stevens, what's gotten into you?"

"Ma, I'm ten years old now. Ten-year-old boys have no business helping out in the kitchen or in the garden. We are the kings of our own kingdoms."

"Where did you hear that nonsense?"

"It's not nonsense, Ma."

"Did you make this up?"

"No ma'am. Clarence Slaughter told me when I ran into him on the way to school today."

Ma sighed. I detected what looked like might have been the beginning of a grin on Ma's face—she couldn't really be smiling at something like this though, could she? "Clarence Slaughter doesn't know beans about what it means to be an obedient child, Johnny."

"Ma ...." I wanted to tell her that if I didn't rebel against housework, Clarence planned to beat me to a pulp. I couldn't bring myself to reveal that my fear of Clarence had motivated my rebellion.

"Yes, Johnny?"

"Ma, I can't cut up the onion."

"How about peeling the potatoes?"

"I can't do that either, Ma."

"What can you do to help for supper, Johnny?"

"I will do what I please, Ma."

"Okay, Johnny, that's fine."

"It is?" I gasped, almost in shock. Ma shed no tears, and she did not lecture me about honoring my parents.

"Sure, Johnny. You don't have to help prepare supper."

This was much easier than I thought it would be. "Ma, I'm going to go fishing for a bit, down by the creek."

"That's fine, Johnny."

As I walked across the yard with my fishing pole, I saw Elias brushing down the horses, a chore that we all shared.

"Where are you going, lazy bones?" asked Elias. "Fishing now? You've done your chores?"

"I'm not doing chores any more unless I want to, Elias."

"Are you crazy, Johnny? Pa's not going to take kindly to your laziness."

"It's not laziness, Elias. I'm just being practical. I've got more important things to do than chores."

"Who told you that lie, Johnny?"

"Clarence Slaughter is the one who convinced me of this."

"Clarence Slaughter? Since when could he convince you of anything?"

Ott walked around the corner of the barn, where he had been watering the fruit trees, and his face broke into a big smile. "Johnny, going down to the fishing hole? Wait 'till Pa hears about this."

"It didn't seem to bother Ma any."

"It was okay with Ma?" asked Ott.

"Yes, she didn't get huffy or have a fit or anything bad like that. She just said it was all right."

"Johnny, I have a question for you," said Elias with a smile.

"Sure, Elias, what is it?"

"Suppose you are the general of an army, and every day you go to battle against the enemy's army."

"I'm with you so far, Elias."

"Good. Now, day in and day out, you fight the enemy. They whoop you sometimes; you whoop them sometimes; but you're almost always in battle."

"Okay, then what?"

"Then one morning, the general of the enemy's army sends you a note that says he's done fighting, he's tired of the war, and that you can come take all the land you want. In fact, he says you can come and do whatever you want. You can have the whole kingdom that he's been trying to defend. What would you think then?"

"I would reckon that I was walking into some kind of trap."

Elias smiled. "Be careful out there, Little General. Ma and Pa may appear easygoing on the surface, but they are formidable foes if you try crossing them."

"Who do you want to read the eulogy at the funeral, Johnny?" questioned Ott.

"What funeral, Ott?"

"Yours, Johnny. I don't expect you to live past tomorrow." Ott chuckled and then went back to watering the fruit trees in the orchard.

I went to the creek, and I got a bite on the first cast. The fish jumped off the hook, though, and I got no bites the rest of the afternoon.

# 21

# Hungry

Then I heard the sound of the supper bell. My stomach growled with hunger, and I knew that Ma's supper would be great as usual. I ran to the house and, with a smile on my face, I opened the door. I stood around the table and started chatting with everybody. I, along with everybody else, stopped chatting the moment Pa joined us.

"You may sit down," said Pa, and we did.

At that moment, I realized that each person at the table had a bowl in front of him, except for me. Each person at the table had a spoon in front of him, except for me. Ma scooped a large helping of vegetable stew for each person, except for me, and she gave each person at the table a large slab of homemade bread, except for me.

Before I said anything, Pa explained, "Johnny, I understand from Ma that you have decided to cease doing chores. That's your choice, but you should know that as long as you are not doing chores, you will not be eating any meals."

He let that sink in for a moment. It had occurred to me that I could just go into the kitchen and fix my own meal.

"Furthermore, Johnny, don't even think about fixing your own meal with food that I have provided. If you're going to eat, you've got to go out and get your own food."

"What?" That caught me off guard.

"And we will let you stay here tonight and perhaps tomorrow night, but if you're not going to do any work, you're not going to stay here."

"Pa, this isn't fair!" I exclaimed.

"Not fair? You have a mother who works hard every day to feed you and mend your clothes and help you with your schoolwork, yet you refuse to help out in little ways like cutting up an onion or peeling some potatoes … and you say it's not fair?"

Pa had a good point there. I was stuck on both sides. I had to choose between disobedience of my parents or getting pummeled by Clarence. I was hoping Pa would let it lie a while so I could think about the situation.

Unfortunately for me, Pa continued. "Now, Johnny, the way I see it, it's entirely your choice as to whether you eat or not, or whether you sleep in the house or out in the field under the stars. But remember this—your mother is your mother, and because she is one of your parents, she is to be honored and obeyed. I will not tolerate disobedience. Come with me."

I knew better than to argue with Pa, even though at that moment I realized what the consequences of my actions were going to be. I wasn't looking forward to this.

Pa led me out back, behind the barn, and he took a switch to my behind. It wasn't a brutal thrashing, but it stung enough that it hurt my pride along with my backside for a couple of days afterward.

The rebellion lasted until the next morning, at which point I decided I didn't want to starve—not only for food, but for my family's love and affection. I got up early—my stomach wouldn't let me sleep—and I did almost all the chores myself before the rest of the family got out of bed. As soon as Ma woke up, I apologized and asked what I could do to help.

Kate had been unusually silent through this whole episode. At breakfast, after I announced that I had surrendered and would again do my share of the chores, Kate, though still sick and feeling tired, asked, "Johnny, do you want me to go beat the stuffin' out of Clarence Slaughter?"

I told her no.

"Johnny," began Pa, "what does Clarence Slaughter have to do with any of this?"

"Well Pa, he thought up the idea."

"The idea for what?"

"He feels that boys should be free from doing household chores so they can enjoy life to the fullest."

"And what happens if you don't go along with what he says?"

"Then he said I would be a 'mama's boy' and that he would beat me to a pulp."

"To a pulp?"

"Yes sir, to a pulp."

"Johnny, we should talk. I'm going into town later in the morning. I want you to ride into town with me," he said softly but firmly. I didn't have a choice in the matter.

At half past eleven, he called for me and headed toward the barn. "Let's hitch up the wagon, son."

We hooked the wagon up to Millie and headed toward town.

"What is it, Pa?"

Pa didn't answer right away. Beads of sweat were rolling off my nose. I sat as still as I could, but the heat and humidity were bearing down on us as we rode the wagon into town.

"It's a scorcher today," said Pa. He appeared deep in thought, and I knew he'd talk when he was good and ready.

We rode for a while. The still air offered no breeze and the dusty road had no shade. We had no way of cooling off under the sun. Sweat flies pestered and tormented the horse, but even she was so hot that she only made a half-hearted attempt at flicking the flies with her tail. Up ahead, the heat seemed to be rolling off the road in glassy waves, and everything behind it shimmered in the blur.

When we were about halfway to town, Pa cleared his throat.

"Johnny, maybe the reason Clarence Slaughter calls you a mama's boy is simply because he is jealous that you are from a close family, plus the fact that you have a mother and he doesn't."

"He doesn't?"

"No. She died in an accident about seven years ago. Clarence's family used to go to church, but after his mother died that changed. His father started spending time—and money—in the saloons and stopped spending time with Clarence. The boy's life pretty much fell apart after his mother's death."

"Oh, Pa," I sighed. "I didn't know."

We rode in silence the rest of the way into town, and Pa pulled up at the general store.

We did the usual at Ledbetter's. Pa handed Mr. Ledbetter a list from Ma, and I looked around the store. He had no dried fruit.

"Candy, Johnny?" asked Mr. Ledbetter. Mrs. Lincoln lay on the counter, trying to stay cool. I stroked her and she purred.

"Oh, no thanks," I replied quietly. An emptiness filled me and it left room for nothing but sadness for Clarence. I couldn't imagine going through childhood without Ma.

A thought occurred to me at that moment. Other people who choose to be mean—are they going through tough times too? Does anyone choose to be a bully just because he's bored? I thought more about it. I couldn't imagine someone trying to be mean just for the sake of being mean.

I wasn't sure what all that meant, except that perhaps I needed to stop being afraid—and judgmental—and start being more of a friend. I suspected that I would have the opportunity to put that into practice soon.

# 22

# A New Friend

"Wait up!" Elias shouted, running toward me from the barn. With Kate still ill, I had begun my walk to school alone.

"What is it, Elias?"

"I'll walk with you to school."

"You'll walk with me? Why?"

"Why? Because Clarence Slaughter is going to beat you to a pulp, that's why. I'm not about to let him do that to a brother of mine."

I stopped and looked at Elias.

"You would do that for me?"

"I would," said Elias, smiling.

"Well, Elias, you won't believe this, but I think I can walk by myself today. I appreciate your offer, but I feel ready to take on Clarence."

"Really?"

"Really. But thanks. It does mean a lot to me."

"Okay, Johnny, whatever you say. But listen, if you do change your mind, today or ever, just let me know and I'll be there for you."

"Got it. Thanks, Elias."

He gave me a light punch on the shoulder and then turned to walk back toward the barn. The day had started well, and I found myself almost looking forward to seeing Clarence.

I whistled as I walked to school, and as I turned at the bend in the trail, I encountered Clarence Slaughter on the path. He was alone.

"Hello," I said in a way that sounded and felt very relaxed to me. I wanted to show Clarence that I wasn't afraid.

"So, Johnny, are you still a mama's boy?"

"Actually Clarence, I did try it for a while Friday night, but it didn't go over so well. The problem was that Pa said if I don't work, I don't eat, and I wouldn't be able to stay in the house."

"You gave in, Johnny. There are consequences to pay, you realize."

"Well, of course. Do what you need to do."

"What? You're going to just accept it and let me beat you up?"

"Look Clarence, I don't want to get hit any more than you do. Beat me up if you really need to. But after that, I have a question for you."

"You have a question for me? Are you sure it's not a plea?"

"No, it's just a question."

"What is it?"

"Aren't you going to beat me up first?"

"I don't know. I might save that for later. Now, what's the question?"

"Well, I wanted to ask you if you'd like to go fishing with me. I usually fish down on the creek and I know a couple of good fishing holes."

Clarence paused. "Johnny, why are you inviting me to fish with you? No one has ever invited me to go fishing."

"I think we can learn a lot from each other, Clarence."

"What can I learn from a little mama's boy?"

"Nothing, maybe. You're probably right. I guess you can go ahead and beat me up now."

"I don't know," sighed Clarence, deflated. "I just don't quite feel like hitting anybody right now."

"Want to go fishing after school, Clarence?"

"Well, um, I guess I'd like to. Let me talk to my father first."

"Will he be all right with it?"

"I think so."

"Just let me know."

"Okay, Johnny."

"Bye, Clarence."

"Bye, Johnny."

I walked on to school, leaving Clarence standing there.

The hours passed slowly. All day long I kept thinking about the conversation with Clarence and how nice it would be for a bully to turn into a friend.

After school, I found Clarence waiting for me on the path. "My father says I can go fishing with you, Johnny." Clarence had a fishing pole with him.

We walked to my house, where we found Pa trying to mend a wagon wheel out in the yard. When Pa saw us walking together he stopped and nodded.

"Pa, is it okay with you if Clarence and I go fishing for a while?"

"Is this part of the Anti Mama's Boy League or whatever it was called?" asked Pa.

Clarence blushed. "No sir, I … well, Johnny just invited me fishing. That is, if it's okay with you."

Pa smiled. "Johnny, I still want you to do your chores before fishing. But then, yes, you can go."

"Yes, Pa."

"Can I help?" asked Clarence. "I figure 'tween the two of us we can knock out any chore pretty quickly."

The two of us worked together to make sure the animals had food and we cleaned up the floor in the barn. Then we headed down to the creek. We fished for nearly two hours. We didn't catch anything, but we talked.

The conversation was awkward at first. We talked about the weather. We talked about dirt. We talked about cows. The more we talked, though, the more I felt that I was talking to an old friend, catching up on life with someone I hadn't seen for a long time.

That night as I lay in bed, I found myself thinking about how my day had begun with expectations of getting pummeled by a guy who, by the day's end, had become a friend.

"Ott? You awake?" I whispered.

"No. But don't let that stop you."

"Isn't it funny," I said, "how surprises can happen when we're not expecting it?"

"You mean like how enemies in the morning can be friends by nightfall?"

"Yes. It was like a miracle."

"I suppose God had something to do with that, don't you think?"

"I think you're right, Ott. It's just amazing how good I feel, knowing I don't have to worry about Clarence any more."

"Maybe you need to worry about life getting too easy," said Ott.

"I don't need to worry about that!" I said.

"Why not?"

"There's always Eugene."

# 23

# Back in School

"Hi, Johnny," said Clarence, standing on the path when Kate and I turned the bend on the way to school the next morning. He looked troubled.

"Hi, Clarence," I said, hoping that he still wanted to be friends.

"Johnny, Kate …." He looked down at his feet as though nervous.

"What is it, Clarence?" I asked.

"Well, I was wonderin' … um, what do you think would happen if … well, it's kind of like this …."

"Jeepers, Clarence, what's on your mind?" blurted Kate.

"Kate, shhh!" I commanded.

"Well," continued Clarence, "Johnny, do you think I could come back to school again?"

"School? Sure Clarence, I don't see why not. You know, though, that this is the last week of school until after harvest."

"I know. My pa wants me to go back to school—in fact, he is pushing me hard to do it—but—"

"Clarence, is this some kind of trick?" interrupted Kate. "Because if it is, I'm going to tan your hide so fast you won't know Tuesday from Friday."

"Kate, please!" I said. "Clarence, you were saying?"

"I'm sayin' that I ain't been in the classroom for two years, and I don't know if I can remember anything, especially my ciphers. I kind of hoped Miss Baines could give me something to work on during the break."

I thought about that a moment.

"Clarence, do you reckon I could work with you a little bit after some school days, just to help you remember how to do things?" I asked.

"Honestly, Johnny, I don't know if I like the thought of you teaching me."

"It would not really be teaching, Clarence. It'd just be jogging your memory."

"Johnny Stevens, that'd be great."

"When do you want to start?"

"Can we start today?"

"Sounds good to me. Come on."

I walked in the classroom, and Clarence followed. Miss Baines gasped when she saw Clarence, and I figured that she thought that Clarence came to cause trouble.

"Miss Baines, I want you to meet my new friend, Clarence Slaughter," I said, smiling. She stood there with her mouth open and her eyes wide with astonishment.

"Miss Baines," I asked, "do you remember Clarence?"

"Why, uh, yes Johnny, of course I remember Clarence," responded Miss Baines.

I had always thought Miss Baines to be unflappable, but this surprise visit by Clarence appeared to rattle her.

Clarence seemed to sense Miss Baines' discomfort with the situation, and he quickly tried to make amends.

"Miss Baines, I … I apologize for my disruptive behavior in the past. I want to come back to school and give learnin' a serious try."

Miss Baines didn't know what to say at first.

"Welcome, Clarence. I'm glad to have you back. We only have a few days left before the harvest break. Does your father know you are back in school?"

"Mostly. We talked about it last night, and he really encouraged me to come back. I know I'm behind in my schoolin' where I ought to be, but Johnny said he is willing to tutor me during the harvest break."

Miss Baines smiled. "I can help tutor you too, Clarence. I'd be more than happy to do that."

Clarence blushed. "Miss Baines, would you really do that?"

"Yes, Clarence, I would do that."

If Clarence's return to school had surprised Miss Baines that morning, she was doubly surprised when Clarence raised his hand in class and attempted to answer a question. The boy had changed, and I suspected we would see more good things from Clarence in days to come.

# 24

# Out of Sight

"Johnny and Sam," Pa whispered, "stay behind the thicket and keep quiet."

Sam and I had been picking blackberries along the creek bank, near the meadow that was on the edge of our farm. Pa, in the meadow, stood on the other side of the blackberry bushes.

Keeping quiet, we obeyed Pa. I wasn't sure what was going on at first, but then I heard a voice call out from across the meadow.

"Stevens," said the voice, obviously belonging to Horace Kilpatrick. A few seconds passed before I heard the voice again.

"Stevens, good to see you," said Mr. Kilpatrick. "Your wife said I would find you out here."

"Horace, how are you today?"

"Stevens, I want to talk with you about something. I have a proposition for you."

"Yes?" said Pa.

"Stevens, you're a farmer, and a good one, and one of the reasons you're a good one is because you are also a good businessman. You have good business sense."

Pa didn't say anything.

"Now, the election for Polk City mayor is coming up, and I intend on running."

Again, Pa didn't say anything.

"I'm running, of course, against Mayor Hickman. Now, I believe that Mr. Hickman is doing a fine job, but I also believe that I would be a far superior choice."

"Well, Horace, I will look at the candidates as thoroughly as I can, and I will vote for the person I think best."

"Stevens, I'm not here to ask you to vote for me, but I … uh … I would like your help and support."

"What do you mean, Horace? Do you want me to ask others to vote for you? If I think you're the most qualified candidate, I'd be happy to—"

"No, no, no, Stevens, that's not it at all."

"What is it then?" asked Pa.

"I understand that you are one of the ballot counters for this year's election."

"Yes, that's right," said Pa.

"I want you to change the results—if they need changing—so that I win the election."

"Horace, what you are suggesting is illegal."

"Stevens, if it's best for the city, I don't see what's wrong with it," snapped Mr. Kilpatrick. Then he seemed to regain his composure, like a cobra trying to lull his prey to sleep before striking, and he spoke in an enticing tone.

"Stevens, look, I've got plans for this city, big plans, and I want you to be part of it. I think these farms that you and Hudson live on will be profitable someday—it's a prime location for business expansion, say a new grist mill—and I want to get started with growing the town. I'll buy the property from your landlord and then sell it back to you at a reasonable price, and then we'll build it up, increasing its value. They're doing the same thing in Des Moines. What does Des Moines have that we don't? Nothing. We

just need an enterprising businessman, and here I am. You and I could be rich men, Stevens. So, are you in?"

"Horace, I will not alter the results."

"You are a man of principles, Stevens, and I admire that. I really do. I'll make this worth your while," said Mr. Kilpatrick with an impatient tone that seemed on the verge of anger.

"Horace, I cannot do it. What you are suggesting is illegal and unethical. Think about it."

"No, you think about it Stevens," snarled Mr. Kilpatrick. "Ride this with me, and you will end up a wealthy man. But if you refuse, you will end up with nothing. Don't cross me, Stevens."

"Horace, I will not do it."

"You … you will regret it. I promise you that," hissed Mr. Kilpatrick. "You haven't heard the last from me, Stevens!" Mr. Kilpatrick stomped away angrily back across the meadow. Sam and I didn't move until Pa whispered that we could come out.

"You heard everything? Did you understand what he said?"

"Yes, Pa."

"Yes, Mr. Stevens," Sam nodded.

"When we get home, I want you boys to write down everything you heard."

"Yes sir."

"Good. Now let me help you get some berries picked."

# 25

# Little Green Apples

We had a small fruit orchard just on the other side of the barn, and we grew about every kind of fruit that could grow in central Iowa. I liked the apple trees the best.

Now, Pa had told us children not to eat the little green apples. I don't know why he didn't just leave it at that, but—like many parents—he felt the need to add some "because" reasons in there. Don't eat the little green apples because it's not good for you. Don't eat the little green apples because you'll get sick. Don't eat the little green apples because you might end up with the "cholera morbus." If Pa had simply left it as, "Don't eat the little green apples," period, that would have been the end of the story. He went on so about how we shouldn't eat the little green apples, and finally curiosity got the best of me.

One mid-August Saturday afternoon, I went out behind the barn, picked one little green apple, and bit into it—sour, but delicious! Quickly, I gathered two handfuls of little green apples, and I ate one right after the other until they were all gone.

I waited a couple of minutes and didn't feel any ill effects. In fact, I felt good, and I figured I probably wasn't going to die. I looked around and didn't see anyone, so I gathered another couple of handfuls of apples and, again, ate them as quickly as I could. I did this two or three more times until I was full and sufficiently satisfied.

I went back into the house and stood in front of the looking glass to see if my appearance had changed. It hadn't. Pa would have no way of knowing that I had eaten all those little green apples.

That night at supper, everything started off fine. Quiet at the supper table as usual, we ate in silence for a few minutes. Suddenly Pa gasped, startling the rest of us. We stared at him.

"Johnny!" said Pa, his voice in a panic. "Oh, Johnny, no. Johnny, how do you feel? Can you hear me? Can you see me? Speak to me, Johnny, oh my youngest son."

"Pa, I feel great. In fact, this might be the best I've ever felt."

Pa looked at me, and then he had a look of horror in his eyes. "Oh my, Johnny, you're looking mighty green there."

"Green?"

"Green. I think you're getting cholera morbus, and it looks like it might be a bad case of it."

"No, Pa, I can't be getting cholera morbus or anything else. I feel fine, really I do."

"Catherine, what do you think. A moment ago, he felt great. Now he only feels fine."

"Oh, John, I'm worried about Johnny. Oh, I hope he doesn't die."

"Pa," asked Elias, "if Johnny dies, what are you going to do with all of his belongings?"

"Belongings? Oh, you mean like his shiny rock collection, his bag of arrowheads, and that coon skeleton that we found in the creek?"

"Exactly. Who gets those, Pa?" asked Elias.

"I reckon we'll give them to somebody who might appreciate them, perhaps Eugene Dinwidden III."

"Should I run and get Eugene so he can pick up the stuff as soon as Johnny goes?" asked Ott.

"Pa, really, I still feel great," I said, not quite as sure about it as I had been earlier.

"Johnny, you're turning greener," added Grandma.

"No question about it," said Pa, "you've got cholera morbus. I can see it in your eyes. I need to get you some of my tonic."

Pa left the table and came back a minute later, bottle and spoon in hand. He uncorked the bottle, poured out a big spoonful, and announced, "This will cure what ails you," as he poured it down my throat.

That stuff made my head shake. On top of that, my throat burned and my eyes were watering.

"Pa, I don't think it's taking yet," said Ott.

"Pa," I sputtered, "I'm doing great."

"Well, that little bit of tonic helped, but you need more to get the rest of the way better."

He poured out another spoonful and in my mouth it went. And then he did a third spoonful, just for good measure.

At this point, my stomach started turning somersaults. I felt sick. I asked to be excused and I went to bed.

Not until sometime later did I learn that Pa had found a pile of apple cores in back of the barn on the very afternoon that I had eaten the apples. I hadn't covered my tracks very well.

It didn't matter that Pa knew what I had done even before administering the tonic. Never again did I touch those little green apples.

# 26

# Ominous Clouds

"Johnny, you didn't have to get all prettied up just to come visit me," laughed Sam.

I admit that I must have been a mess. I was soaked in sweat and my arms were covered with dirt. I had been outside doing chores and helping Pa all morning on that hot September day. The day was about as hot and sultry as it could get, one of those days where, if I went to the cellar to retrieve something for Ma, I would just want to stay down there, breathing in the cool air.

"You're one to talk, Sam Hudson. You look like a raccoon, or maybe you put on your war paint this morning."

Sam was dripping with sweat, and his brown-streaked face revealed where he had tried to wipe away the moisture with dirt-caked fingers.

"Done with chores?" asked Sam.

"Yep. You?"

"Yep. Race you up the hill, Johnny!"

Sam took off in a dead sprint. I followed, soon catching and passing him. I didn't look up until the ground started flattening out. We were huffing and puffing by the time we reached the top.

"Whew, Johnny, you're too fast for me today. I'm going to have to ask your pa to start giving you more—"

"Sam, look!" I pointed west, over the valley below. Off in the distance, several miles away, there were dark storm clouds, and they were headed this way. Rain! It looked like we might be in for rain!

"Woo hoo!" Sam shouted. "I'm going to go tell Father."

"I'll go tell Pa. See you, Sam!"

"Bye, Johnny!"

I raced home as fast as my legs would carry me. I found Pa in the barn.

"Pa! West! Look west!"

Pa stepped out of the barn and looked. Sure enough, the clouds were just peeking over the top of the slope.

"Pa, it's going to rain!"

"Oh mercy," said Pa softly. "There's something coming, and I'm not sure it's just rain."

"What's wrong, Pa? We need rain."

"Yes, we do, son, but the last time I saw something like this, we ended up with a hail storm." The wind blowing in our faces felt good, and as we were standing there it seemed to pick up speed and drop in temperature. "I hope I'm wrong, Johnny. Come on!"

Pa ran toward the house. "Catherine, children!" he called from the yard. "Big storm coming. Might be hail!"

George, Elias, and Ott came running out of the barn; Ma and Kate came out of the house.

Pa barked out orders: "Johnny, put Constance in the center of the barn under the loft; tie up Millie and Billy next to her. Ollie should be okay where she is. George and Elias, take the larger pieces of unchopped wood from the wood pile and stand them up on-end in Ma's garden, along the rows and between rows. Ott, get the old tarp out of the barn—the one we used for the church meeting last year— and lay it gently on top of the garden. Then pin the edges down with firewood." Pa wanted to preserve Ma's garden.

"Kate," Pa continued, "round up the chickens and put them in the barn. Catherine, collect our valuables in the house and put them in the cellar. I'll make sure Mother gets in the cellar and then I'll help you."

The storm was coming in quickly. The taste of rain drops was in the air, but Pa was right ... there was something ominous about this storm.

The wind whistled through the big tree in the side yard, but there was a deeper noise, a more threatening rumble, that sounded like an army marching toward us from somewhere over the horizon.

I could see the clouds billowing over the slope toward us, but I still couldn't see the rain. I could hear the rain though—or rain and ice—as it came pounding down behind the slope, hurtling downward from the heavens, intent on crushing everything in its path.

And then I saw it—not the gray sheet that I usually saw as a rain storm approached across the plains, but a white sheet of hail leaving a trail of ice and destruction; ice balls as large as my fist were coming down, striking the earth and hammering dents in the ground.

"To the cellar!" Pa yelled, and we ran to the root cellar, getting inside and closing the door before the first pieces of hail could find us. Elias had Old Jack down there with us. Kate had brought down both cats.

Pa heaved a deep sigh, but then the hail began striking the cellar door with a fury that sounded as though someone were outside, trying to break in with an ax.

The hail pounded on the cellar door for what felt like an hour but probably was only twenty minutes or maybe even less. Each hail stone that hit the door exploded in a loud CRACK!

"You know what we haven't done yet?" said Pa. "We haven't prayed."

"Pa, I've been praying the whole time," Kate said softly.

Pa looked at Kate and then picked her up, hugged her, and said, "That's my little girl. The rest of us should be praying too."

"Listen!" commanded Elias.

We listened. There was no noise, no sound at all. The hail had ceased, stopping all at once in a sudden hush. Pa immediately opened the cellar door and we stepped outside.

The ground was blanketed with white; at first glance it almost looked like a snowstorm had come through, only it wasn't smooth like snow.

"No," whispered Pa. "It can't be." He looked stunned. He knelt down on the ground and, at a loss for words, picked up a chunk of ice the size of a large tomato.

"Pa, I'll check the house," said George.

"Elias and I will look at the field," said Ott. "Come on, Elias!"

George stepped inside the house while Elias and Ott ran, slipped, stumbled, and slid their way across the yard to the field to assess the damage. I could see them from a distance as they dug down into the ice, I guess so they could figure out how deep it was.

George emerged from the house a minute or two later with his report. "The windows are shattered, but the rest of the house looks okay."

Elias and Ott returned from the field.

"Pa," said Ott, "We lost maybe half of the corn and all the beans. We've got almost three inches of ice over most of the field."

"Well, you know what?" said Pa, standing up and surprising us all by having a hint of a smile on his face.

"What, Pa?" asked Kate.

"The Lord is in charge of this place, just like he's in charge of our lives. He knows what he is doing. I don't know why this happened—I really thought our prayers were going to rescue the farm—but for some reason God didn't want an abundant crop this year."

"Pa?" asked Kate.

"What is it, little one?"

"Pa, I know why the crops were destroyed."

"Why was that, Kate?"

"Because I didn't pray for the crops. I felt I should pray for the important things—I prayed that none of us would be hurt, and I prayed that the animals would all be safe. The animals!" Kate made her way over to the barn, as quickly as she could on the ice. She opened the door and went inside, and then she came back out a minute later.

"Hey, they're all fine!" she shouted. "They're safe! But the barn has a big hole in the roof."

"We do have much to be thankful for," said Ott with a smile.

"Amen," said Pa.

# 27

# Clarence and Eugene

"Are there any volunteers to come to the board and do some multiplication for us?" asked Miss Baines, on our first day back in school in mid-October after the harvest break.

Clarence's hand shot up, and it was understandable in a sense. He and I had been working on multiplication during the harvest break, and he was gaining confidence. The problem was that what we had been working on were the multiplication tables, not solving harder problems.

"Clarence, no," I whispered, but it was too late. Miss Baines saw Clarence's hand waving vigorously.

"Clarence, thank you for volunteering. Please come to the board."

Clarence walked up front with a smile on his face. He didn't know what was in store for him. Miss Baines had worked with him on history and English, but not math. She didn't know what he could or could not do.

"Clarence, please solve this problem for us: seven hundred sixty-eight times forty-seven."

Clarence stood there, and never have I seen a face lose a smile and go from normal to pale white to bright red so quickly, all in about five seconds.

The classroom was silent; I suspected that nearly every student in that room was saying a silent prayer for Clarence at that time.

The silence was broken by a snicker from the back of the room. Miss Baines looked back; I looked back; most of the class looked back; and the worst part was that Clarence looked back. It was Eugene.

The old Clarence would have gotten angry; perhaps the new Clarence felt angry too. Clarence didn't show it though—instead, he showed embarrassment. I wanted to rescue him, but I didn't know how in that situation. I couldn't really walk up to the front and do the problem with him—or could I?

Not sure what I was going to do, my hand went up anyway. Miss Baines looked at me. "Yes, Johnny?"

"May I come up and help Clarence?" I asked. "I know he knows his multiplication tables, but he hasn't solved a math problem like this in a couple of years." Truth be known, I didn't know if Clarence had ever solved a problem like this.

"Yes, Johnny. You're welcome to come up to the board."

I walked up front, looking at Clarence. He had a quizzical look on his face, as though he were asking, "How are you going to get me out of this mess?"

When I reached him, I whispered, "You can do this."

I wrote seven hundred sixty-eight on the board, and under it I wrote forty-seven. "Okay, Clarence, first we take the eight and the seven. Now, you do know what eight times seven is, right?"

Clarence paused. "Oh please," I thought to myself, "you do know this."

Clarence continued pausing for a few seconds before blurting out, "Fifty-six!"

"Very good, Clarence," I said. I then explained how to write down the six and carry the five over to the tens column; I even explained why it was done that way. I walked him through the whole problem, and by the time we finished, I knew that he understood both the process and why it worked the way it did.

"Johnny," said Miss Baines, "that was as good an explanation on how to do multiplication as I have ever heard."

I blushed. "Thank you, Miss Baines."

"Thanks, Johnny," whispered Clarence as we both walked back to our desks.

Eugene was still laughing, softly under his breath. Clarence glared at him.

"Clarence," I whispered, "ignore Eugene. He acts like this to everybody."

"Eugene," said Miss Baines, "please come to the board."

"Me? But I didn't raise my hand!" said Eugene.

"Apparently you are comfortable doing these multiplication problems. Come to the board."

Eugene reluctantly stood up. I had never quite seen this side of Miss Baines before. When Eugene was at the board, Miss Baines said, "Eight hundred twenty-nine times sixty-seven."

Eugene turned red. He wrote the numbers down slowly.

"Miss Baines, I have a bad headache. Can I sit down?" he whined.

"No, you may not, Eugene."

"But Mother says I have apoplexy or something and that I should not be put under stress. She will not be happy when she hears about this."

"Eugene, she will not be happy when she hears about how you have been behaving toward others in this class. You will not sit down until you do this problem."

Eugene stood there for a moment, squirming, trying to figure out how to get started. He apparently had not been paying too much attention when I was helping Clarence.

"Eugene appears to be struggling," Miss Baines announced to the class. "Is there anyone who would like to come up and help him?" She was looking with a twinkle in her eye at Clarence.

Clarence stared at her. He pointed to himself and silently mouthed, "Me?"

Miss Baines nodded.

Clarence raised his hand. "Miss Baines, I'll try to help Eugene."

"Thank you, Clarence."

Clarence stood up and came to the board. Eugene was scowling. Clarence held out his hand, and Eugene handed him the chalk. Clarence began.

"Now, Eugene, first you have to take seven times nine. What is that?"

"Fifty-six. No, wait. Seventy-two."

Clarence remained silent, staring at Eugene.

"Well, what is it then, if it's not seventy-two?" demanded Eugene.

"It's sixty-three, Eugene. So you write down the three in the ones column, and carry a six to the tens column."

Clarence continued through the whole problem. He did it perfectly. Eugene, embarrassed and put back in his proper place, was quiet the rest of the afternoon.

"I don't know how long I can refrain from beating him to a pulp," sighed Clarence as we were walking home.

"You did even better than that, Clarence, when you helped him with that math problem. I don't think Eugene will ever bother you again."

# 28

# Mr. Shanley

I heard the hooves of a horse racing into the yard at breakneck speed. I stuck my head outside the barn door—it was Elias, and he was riding Billy about as fast as she would go.

He brought the horse into the barn, and then he ran toward the house with me trailing right behind.

"Pa," he called out. "Pa!"

Pa stepped out of the house. "What is it, Elias?"

"Pa, it's … it's Mr. Shanley."

"What about Mr. Shanley?" said Pa.

"Mr. … Mr. Shanley is … he's … he's going … going back east." Elias was having trouble catching his breath.

"Slow down, Elias. Slow down," said Pa in a firm but steady voice, almost as if trying to calm a wild horse.

Elias took a deep breath, and then another.

"There, that's better," said Pa. "Now, tell me what's happening?"

"Well, I was at C.W. Burt's place, returning a saddle I had repaired. All I know is that Mr. Burt says that Mr. Shanley has family that is sick in Philadelphia and he is moving back to take care of them."

Pa flinched ever so slightly.

"What's going to happen, Pa? Will we have to move?" asked Elias.

"I don't know," said Pa, scratching his chin. "I just don't know."

That afternoon, there was a knock on the door. It was Mr. Shanley. Pa invited him in and he sat down at the table.

"John, I wanted you to hear first, but word sneaked out."

"I heard pieces of it, Tom. Family illness?"

"That's the heart of it, John. My mother is dying and they need my help. Coincidentally, a week ago I was approached by Kilpatrick. He gave me an offer on all my property."

"Kilpatrick wants to buy all your property?"

"He does. I own four farms, and he wants them all."

"Was his offer fair?"

"The offer is considerably less than the land is worth, but I'm really itching to get back and help the family. I wanted to give you the first chance at buying this farm from me. Honestly, having the cash now would be nice, but I'd like to sell it for what it's worth, or close to it."

"Tom, I can't afford to pay what the farm is worth, and I doubt that I can match Kilpatrick's offer."

"Well, between you and me, Kilpatrick is offering two hundred dollars for this farm. I can't sell it for that, but I would be willing to take five hundred for it, from you only."

Pa scratched his chin and he looked at Ma.

"Tom, that's kind of you. I know the property is worth considerably more than that. Tell you what. Before I make a decision on that, let me think about it. Can I get back to you tomorrow?"

"Sure, John. That sounds good. I'll hold off Kilpatrick for another day."

Mr. Shanley stood up. "I really want this to work out in whatever way is best for you, John."

"I know, Tom, and I appreciate that. Good night."

"Good night, John, Mrs. Stevens," he nodded, heading out the door.

It was quiet that evening at the supper table. Pa was thinking, and so was Ma.

"It's just not right. Kilpatrick is leveraging someone else's misfortune so that he can acquire land at a low price. It's not illegal, but it sure feels unethical to me," said Pa.

"I wish we could help Tom somehow," said Ma.

Finally, Ott asked, "So are we going to buy the farm from Mr. Shanley?"

Pa looked at Ma, and in unison they responded, "No."

"Why not?" asked Kate. "Does that mean we have to move?"

"First of all, it would take every cent we own to pay Mr. Shanley a fair price for his farm. The hail storm pretty much washed away any earnings for this year. Now, as to whether we will move, I do not know the answer to that yet. It certainly is an option. Homesteading land is still available out in Kansas and Nebraska."

Homesteading—I had heard about that. The government was giving away free land to help encourage settlers to go to the West. It would mean starting a farm all over again, but it would be a farm that we owned.

"Pa, but all our friends are here," I said.

"Johnny, you children will be able to make friends wherever you go. But I have not said yet that we are moving."

"I don't want to move," said Kate, pouting.

"Kate," said Ma sternly, "that's enough about this for now."

We ate the rest of the meal in silence, wondering what we were going to do. When it came right down to it, I didn't like the thought of moving at all. Suddenly, I didn't feel all that adventurous. I just wanted to stay in Polk City.

# 29

# Selling the Farm

The next day, Pa and I took the wagon into Polk City. We stopped at the Shanley's house, where we were surprised to find Mr. Horace Kilpatrick.

"Stevens," said Mr. Kilpatrick with a smile. "Shanley here tells me that he has offered you the opportunity to buy your little farm. I am here to tell Shanley that I will pay him twice the amount that you are willing to pay."

Pa glanced at Mr. Shanley and then at Mr. Kilpatrick, before turning back and looking hard into Mr. Shanley's eyes.

"Tom, I am prepared to pay you eight hundred dollars for that property."

Mr. Kilpatrick gasped, "Eight hundred dollars?"

"Eight hundred dollars," said Pa.

"It's not worth anywhere near that, Stevens," said Mr. Kilpatrick.

"Of course it is, Horace. Your offer of two hundred dollars isn't right."

"You cannot possibly afford eight hundred dollars, Stevens," said Mr. Kilpatrick.

"Yes, I can. Have you ever heard of something called savings, Horace?"

"Well, if you've been saving it, Stevens, you haven't been saving it in my bank."

"That's right, Horace."

"Tom, I'll offer you one thousand for the farm," said Mr. Kilpatrick.

Pa cleared his throat. "Horace, a moment ago I heard you say you would offer him twice my offer. Are you backing down?"

Mr. Kilpatrick's face turned red. "I refuse to pay one thousand six hundred dollars for this piece of property. That's highway robbery, Stevens. Now, Shanley, about the rest of your property, I think we can still go ahead and proceed with that transaction."

"I'm still not sure, Horace," said Mr. Shanley. "That's a pretty low price you're offering."

"Well, I think it's fair," said Mr. Kilpatrick. "You want to leave town, and this way you can tie up your loose ends all at once and be done with it."

"You have a point there," said Mr. Shanley.

"Tom, I would be happy to manage the sale of your properties for you, in your absence," said Pa. "That way you wouldn't need to unload the property so cheap."

"You would do that for me?" asked Mr. Shanley.

"I would," said Pa.

"Stevens! I'm warning you, stay out of this," shouted Mr. Kilpatrick.

"Horace, I need another day to think about this," said Mr. Shanley.

"You've meddled too far, Stevens. Shanley, let me know by eight o'clock Monday morning. Good day," said Mr. Kilpatrick, storming out the front door of the house.

A young man walked in the front door as Mr. Kilpatrick was leaving. He looked a bit agitated.

"Mr. Shanley?" said the man.

"Yes?" replied Mr. Shanley.

"Telegram for you, sir," said the man, handing Mr. Shanley a slip of paper.

"Thank you," said Mr. Shanley, sitting down to read the telegram. The man nodded and quickly left through the front door.

Putting his head in his hands, Mr. Shanley breathed a deep sigh. "Well, this changes things," he said quietly.

"What do you mean, Tom?" asked Pa.

"Read this," said Mr. Shanley, handing the telegram to Pa.

Pa read it aloud, softly. "Mother died last night. Moving to Polk City. February. Jeanette." There was silence for a minute or two as both Pa and Mr. Shanley were figuring out what this meant. "Sorry about the news, Tom. Is Jeanette your sister?" asked Pa.

"Yes sir," replied Mr. Shanley.

We talked a while more, but it was clear that Mr. Shanley would be staying in Polk City.

# 30

# Mr. Kilpatrick

The wagon trudged slowly along as we were coming home from church the next day.

"Pa?" asked Kate.

"Yes, Kate?"

"Is Mr. Kilpatrick a neighbor?"

"Yes, I suppose he is."

"Well, you and Ma never seem very happy when you are talking about him."

Pa's face turned red.

"Fair enough," said Pa. "Even adults have trouble figuring out neighbors sometime. I guess that's something I need to keep working on, loving neighbors as God commands. I haven't been thinking good thoughts about Mr. Kilpatrick lately, and I should. He's a neighbor just like anyone else."

Ott spoke up. "Well, he owns much of the neighborhood, but does that make him a neighbor?"

"Ott, you know better than that," Pa replied. "Of course he's a neighbor."

When Pa led the wagon off the road and into the yard, we had a surprise waiting for us. A horse and buggy were near the front porch, and on the porch were two people—Grandma and Mr. Kilpatrick. They were sitting far apart.

Mr. Kilpatrick looked pale and a bit anxious. Grandma was pointing Pa's rifle at him. Old Jack was sitting at Grandma's feet, alert and ready.

Pa brought the wagon to a stop and walked quickly up to the house. "What's going on here?"

Grandma began speaking first. "I was sitting by the fireplace doing my daily prayers when I heard footsteps coming up the porch. I wasn't expecting any visitors, so I grabbed the gun and kept it by my side, and then—"

Mr. Kilpatrick interrupted Grandma. "I knocked on the door, heard no answer, so I entered the house to see if anybody was home."

"And Old Jack didn't try to stop you?" asked Pa, with an incredulous look on his face.

Mr. Kilpatrick's face turned red. "I should have that dangerous dog taken away. Yes, he tried to attack me."

"Until you beat him with your walking stick," retorted Grandma. "I looked out the window in time to see that, and that's when I raised the gun. So this man entered the house, scaring me half to death," Grandma continued, "and of course I'm going to point the gun at him until help gets here. Thank goodness, you've arrived."

"Stevens, tell her to point that gun somewhere else. That thing is liable to go off by accident."

"Go off? This thing ain't even loaded, Mister," said Grandma with a laugh.

"Not loaded?" asked Mr. Kilpatrick in disbelief.

"Right. See this?" Grandma pointed the gun down on the deck and pulled the trigger. A loud CRACK! exploded in the otherwise quiet afternoon, and Grandma was so startled that she dropped the rifle on the ground.

Mr. Kilpatrick fell to the ground the moment the gun fired and then got back up rather sheepishly. "I could have you arrested for threatening me, Mrs. Shideler."

"You'll have a hard time with that, Horace," said Pa, "considering you tried entering the house. No judge will go for that."

"You don't know my connections, Stevens," sneered Mr. Kilpatrick. "I could put away Grandma for a long, long time."

"I'm sorry, John, I didn't realize the gun was loaded," said Grandma apologetically.

"Mother, I always keep my guns loaded. Now Horace," said Pa, turning toward Mr. Kilpatrick, "you were trespassing." Pa spoke calmly but firmly. There was no anger in his voice, but it was a voice of authority and confidence.

"Listen Stevens, the real reason I'm out here is to talk about buying this property. I've been thinking it over and I really want the land. I'll offer you whatever you paid Shanley, plus two hundred dollars."

"He hasn't sold it to me yet, Horace."

"He hasn't?"

"He's not going to. He's staying in Polk City."

"Well, we'll see about that," snapped Mr. Kilpatrick, "but I'm warning you, Stevens, stay out of this. It's between Shanley and me," he said with a snarl. "Good day," said Mr. Kilpatrick, storming off the porch before riding away in his buggy.

Later that afternoon, as I was playing out in the yard with Kate, she said, "Some adults seem so mean, don't they?"

"Like Mr. Kilpatrick?"

"Like Mr. Kilpatrick."

"Maybe that's why people move sometimes, Kate. They want to get away from people like Mr. Kilpatrick."

"I feel sorry for him, Johnny."

"Me too, Kate. I don't think he has any friends."

"I hope he does someday, Johnny. It would be terribly lonely without friends."

"I don't know if he has time for friends, Kate."

"Then what does he do with his time?"

"I guess he just counts his money and tries to think of ways to get more money."

"It's sad."

"Yes, isn't it?"

# 31

# The Tustle

A couple of weeks after we had returned from the harvest break, Miss Baines gave us each the assignment of writing a report about nature, due on that Friday, and it would include reading the report in front of the class. She said we should write about something we were familiar with, so I decided to do a report about turtles.

I worked hard, starting on it right away and spending some time with it each night. I was proud of the work I had done, and I thought the report was turning out well. On Thursday, I asked Ma and Pa to read it to make sure I didn't have any spelling or grammar errors. Both Ma and Pa told me that my handwriting was good except that whenever I would write an "r" it always looked like an "s." Miss Baines had told me that before, too, and she knew I was working on it.

Kate wrote her report about frogs, and together we walked to school on that Friday, excited about our reports.

When we got to the schoolyard, Eugene was already there, and he didn't look too happy.

"What's wrong, Eugene?" asked Kate. "Ready to give your report?"

"Report? Oh, sure," replied Eugene.

"What is your report on, Eugene?" asked Kate.

"On? Uh, it's a surprise."

"A surprise?"

"Yep, a surprise. Oh, Johnny. Did you see the deer antler next to the path?"

"Deer antler?"

"Yep, it had seven points. I think it's from what you would call a fourteen point buck."

"Seven! I've got to see this. Where is it exactly?"

"Go back on the path until it intersects with the trail that goes to the Miller place. Take a right there, and you'll see it in twenty or thirty feet."

"Kate, I'll be right back. I can get there and back in about five minutes."

Eugene said, "Johnny, I'll take your books in for you."

"Thanks Eugene! Okay, be right back."

I sprinted down the path, following Eugene's directions perfectly. I took a right on the trail to the Miller farm, but the antler was nowhere to be found. I ran back to the school and stepped inside, finding Eugene.

"Eugene, I followed your directions perfectly. There was no antler anywhere, as far as I could see."

"Hmm, I don't know then. I wonder if someone, or perhaps an animal, carried it somewhere."

"Okay, children, it's time to get started," said Miss Baines. "Today we will hear your reports. Now, who would like to be first?"

Eugene's hand shot up in the air. I always became suspicious when he volunteered for anything.

"Yes, Eugene, could you please come to the front and read your report to us?"

"Yes ma'am," said Eugene, smiling.

Eugene walked to the front, carrying his report. He cleared his throat and began.

"The Tustle," he stated, reading the title.

"The Tustle?" I thought to myself. What on earth was a tustle?

Eugene continued. "The tustle is an unusual animal. Capable of living both on land and in the sea, the tustle is highly adaptable to its habitat."

Eugene was reading my report! I quickly opened my notebook, where I had put my report. The report was gone—that's because Eugene was holding it in his hands.

Eugene cleared his throat again. He made the mistake of looking at me. I glared at him. I was trying to decide what to do. Was this one of those "turn the other cheek" opportunities, or did Miss Baines need to be told?

I struggled with that for a while, but I also was getting worried about the fact that I no longer had a report to give.

Eugene continued on, telling us about the tustle. He apparently was reading my "r" letters as though they were "s" letters. I looked over at Miss Baines, and I could see that she was turning beet red and she kept wiping her eyes. She looked like she was shaking a little, kind of like you do when you really have to cough but you try as hard as you can to hold it in.

"The box tustle is common, but the most well-known tustle is the snapping tustle. A snapping tustle is capable of biting off a man's *finges*, so be cautious if you find this kind of tustle."

Finges?

By this time, most of the class realized that Eugene really was talking about turtles, not tustles.

"Tustles have a shell on the outside and a soft body on the inside. The tustle uses its shell to defend against its enemies."

The students were snickering. Eugene was red-faced and clearly flustered. I looked at him and he looked at me.

Boy, did he look mad, but there was nothing he could do. He couldn't admit that he had stolen my report and was reading it in front of the class.

"Class! Class! Please settle down and behave. Let Eugene finish telling us about the tustle." I don't know how Miss Baines was able to say that without laughing. Miss Baines was a sharp one, though. Even without anything being said by me, she figured out what had happened.

When Eugene had finished, Miss Baines walked up to my desk, leaned over, and whispered, "Johnny, do you have your report?"

"No ma'am," I truthfully said. "I did have it when I walked to school, but somehow it's gone."

"Johnny, did you write a report about turtles?"

"Yes ma'am."

"Thank you, Johnny."

Eugene didn't hear all of that discussion, and I don't know what Miss Baines said to Eugene exactly. I do know that he had to give another report in class on Monday. His report wasn't about tustles.

# 32

# Relapse

"We caught some fish!" I announced proudly as I stepped into the house after a chilly Saturday morning of fishing in the creek with Clarence and Sam.

I heard a hacking, wheezing cough. Then I noticed that the door to Ma and Pa's room was open, and I saw Ma, Pa, George, and Elias kneeling next to Grandma's bed, in prayer. Kate and Ott were sitting by the fireplace, quietly watching the flames.

"Grandma!" I cried, running to her. "What happened?"

"She's had a relapse, Johnny. I think she's got pneumonia. Her lungs are slowly filling up."

I took Grandma's hand. "Grandma, this is Johnny."

Grandma opened her eyes and smiled.

"Johnny," she whispered, "(cough … cough) let me feel your cheeks."

I gave her a hug and put my cheek next to hers.

"I love feeling (cough) your cheeks (cough) when they're cold, Johnny. Is it cold outside? I'll warm them up for you, Johnny."

She broke into a string of coughing—not a little cough as a person with a scratchy throat may do, but a deep-down, body-shaking cough that hurts from head to toe. She almost appeared to be gagging or choking.

A lump formed in my throat and tears filled my eyes. I left the room with a cloud of sadness hanging over my head.

Ma stepped out of the room immediately after I did.

"What can we do?" I asked, almost feeling panicky.

"We're doing what we can do, Johnny. We're praying."

"Isn't there more? She's my grandma."

"Johnny, she's my mother," said Ma. "Believe it or not, I might love her even more than you do. I just don't think she's going to make it this time. She's ready—I can see it in her eyes."

"No, Ma, that can't be true," I cried. I turned and ran outside, sobbing.

Pa came looking for me a few minutes later. He found me in the barn.

"Johnny?"

"Pa, where's God? If there is a God, why doesn't he heal Grandma?"

"Johnny, either we believe in God or we don't. If we do believe, then we know that there's a better life after this one, one where there will be no more pain and suffering. Grandma will be right where she wants to be, worshiping God."

"And if we don't believe?"

"If we don't believe, then life is meaningless."

"Life doesn't feel meaningless to me, Pa."

"Nor does it to me, Johnny. There's more to life than the few short years we live here on this planet."

"I know, I know. But if she dies, I'll miss her so much."

"Me too, Johnny. We all will. But everyone's got a time when he must go. Think of it this way, Johnny. Eternal life is a long, long time."

"Hundreds of years?"

"Millions of years, just for starters. So seventy or eighty years here really isn't very much."

"I guess you're right. But I'll miss her, just the same."

"I know, Johnny. Why don't you go in and pray with her while you still can."

"Pa, why does it seem like prayer is always the last resort? It's the thing we do when there's nothing left to try," I said. "It's like we're giving up."

"No, Johnny. You've got it backwards. Prayer should be the first thing we do, the most important thing."

"What do we do if the prayer isn't answered?"

"I think the prayer is always answered, Johnny. It's just that sometimes the answer is 'no' or maybe 'not yet.'"

"It's hard, Pa."

"I know it is, son. Now, why don't you go back in there and pray for her."

I did. It was agonizing for me at first, thinking about the possibility of her not being there. But the more I prayed, the bigger the smile she seemed to have on her face—and the more my heart was warmed.

Grandma died two days later, in her sleep. She was at peace at last, free from the torturous, body-wrenching coughing. We all missed her after that, and sometimes thinking of her still makes me cry. Usually, though, when I imagine her up in heaven cackling with God, that puts a smile in my heart. Besides, I know I'll see her again, someday, when it's my turn.

# 33

# Sheriff Cogswell

Sometimes it takes a difficult event like death or some other tragedy to help us keep everything in perspective, to help us remember what's important and what's not. Some folks never find that perspective in the first place.

The Polk City election for mayor was held the following week. Mayor Hickman was elected to serve again, and I knew that Mr. Kilpatrick would not be too pleased about that. I just hadn't realized how important it really was to him.

About a week after the election, Pa and I were out in the barn when a buggy driven by Mr. Kilpatrick, followed by Sheriff Cogswell on his horse, pulled into the yard.

"Hello, Sheriff, Horace," said Pa. "What can we do for you?"

"Hello, John," said the sheriff. Ma walked out onto the front porch at that moment. "Catherine," said the sheriff, nodding toward Ma.

Mr. Kilpatrick stepped out of his buggy.

"Stevens, you are through. Sheriff Cogswell, I want that man arrested immediately!"

"Arrested?" exclaimed Ma. "Whatever for?"

"For falsifying the election results, that's what for," snapped Mr. Kilpatrick.

Pa sighed. "Horace, you should know better than this. Johnny, go get it."

I knew what Pa was talking about. I went inside the house and returned with the piece of paper on which Sam and I had carefully recorded the entire conversation that took place between Pa and Mr. Kilpatrick near the blackberry patch.

"Hand it to the sheriff," said Pa.

I did as directed. The sheriff read the paper.

"Horace, I could have you arrested," said Pa.

"Me? Why?" said Mr. Kilpatrick.

"Horace," said Pa, "when you approached me the other day, one of my children and a friend of his happened to be down in the creek, overhearing everything you said."

"That's eavesdropping, Stevens. You should have told me somebody else was listening when ...." He stopped, red-faced and flustered. "Sheriff, are you going to believe the words of children who say that I told Stevens to throw the election?"

"How did you know that's what the document said, Horace?" asked Sheriff Cogswell.

Mr. Kilpatrick was at a loss for words.

"Horace," continued the sheriff, "I know the Stevens children. I've watched them grow up. And to be honest, I'll take their word over yours any day."

"Never mind. I'll drop the charges," growled an exasperated Mr. Kilpatrick.

"John, Catherine, I'm sorry to trouble you this morning," said Sheriff Cogswell.

"Sheriff, thanks," said Pa.

As Mr. Kilpatrick and Sheriff Cogswell walked out the door, I overhead the sheriff saying, "Kilpatrick, I'm going to be watching your every move from now on. One false step and you're going to prison."

Pa sighed.

"Is Mr. Kilpatrick going to try to get even with you, Pa?" asked Ott.

"I don't know, son. I think Sheriff Cogswell will keep him in his place. I do know that we need to keep Mr. Kilpatrick in our prayers. He's a troubled man." Pa looked at me and said, "Mr. Kilpatrick is an example of what can happen when you don't learn how to make friends as a child. Someone should have befriended Mr. Kilpatrick the way Johnny did with Clarence."

"Pa, maybe it's not too late for Mr. Kilpatrick," I suggested.

"Maybe, Johnny. Maybe," said Pa.

# 34

# Thanksgiving

"It was so kind of you to invite us over for Thanksgiving dinner," said Mr. Slaughter.

"And it was kind of you to accept," replied Pa.

Mr. Slaughter smiled and said, "John, Catherine, I cannot begin to thank you enough for the hospitality and friendship that your children—and yourselves—have given to Clarence, and in turn to me."

"To you?" asked Ma.

"The way I see it," said Mr. Slaughter, "Johnny befriended Clarence, even after Clarence's bullying behavior. I suspect that your son's actions were a reflection of your encouragement to treat Clarence like a ... a friend." Mr. Slaughter had a tear in his eye.

"Ernest," said Pa, "Johnny was merely doing what God asks us to do."

"Maybe so," said Mr. Slaughter, "but not everybody does what God asks them to do. Anyway, I just want to thank you. I'm with my son and your wonderful family. Thanksgiving for me, this year, is special."

"It is for me too, Father," said Clarence with a smile.

"Johnny, Kate, will you help me carry over the food?" asked Ma.

Kate and I carried over a feast, including generous portions of roasted potatoes, green beans, corn, biscuits, and two platters, one with pheasant and the other with venison.

"Catherine, you outdid yourself," said Pa. "This is truly magnificent."

"Indeed, it is, Mrs. Stevens," agreed Mr. Slaughter.

"Well, I'm looking forward to trying the pie you brought over, Mr. Slaughter," said Ma.

Mr. Slaughter and Clarence looked at each other and smiled.

"Do you want to tell them, Clarence?" asked Mr. Slaughter.

"Tell us what?" asked Kate.

"Well, this was going to be a surprise, but I baked the pie," said Clarence.

"You baked a pie?" I asked.

"I did," admitted Clarence.

"It's a beautiful pie, Clarence," said Ma. "If it tastes half as good as it looks, I can't wait."

Clarence blushed. "Thank you, Mrs. Stevens."

"Clarence learned to bake pies from Miss Baines. She taught him more than history in those after-school sessions," said Mr. Slaughter. Then he started laughing. "Johnny and Kate, you look shocked."

"We didn't know Clarence could cook," I replied.

"I was hoping I could find the right way to say, 'Thank you,' at Thanksgiving," smiled Clarence.

Now Ma had tears in her eyes.

"We do have much to be thankful for," she said.

"And with that," said Pa, "let's pray." He said a grace that was appropriate for the occasion—not showy, not boastful, but grateful and filled with a heart of thanksgiving.

We ate in silence for several minutes, not for lack of anything to talk about but because the food was so good.

Finally, Mr. Slaughter spoke up. "So John, what did you think about the election results?"

Pa cleared his throat. "Well, as one of the ballot counters, I'm not really free to say whether I was happy or disappointed in the outcome."

"I understand. I'll tell you, though, I sure am happy that Kilpatrick did not win the election. I don't think that man has an ounce of goodness anywhere in his body."

"I don't know, Ernest," said Pa. "I hope he turns around someday."

"Me too," agreed Mr. Slaughter. "Can someone who is that focused on money really turn around?"

"My inclination is to say no, but that's really between God and him."

"I guess we just wait and see."

"I guess that's what we need to do."

# 35

# Christmas Pageant

"Imagine that—a Stevens can sing!" blurted Mrs. Jacobs, the minister's wife, before covering her mouth when she realized the inappropriateness of her remark.

I could hardly blame her. Mrs. Jacobs usually sat on the opposite side of the church from where we sat, so although she was familiar with Pa's singing, she probably didn't know whether we children could sing.

Apparently she was pleasantly surprised at the first rehearsal for the school's Christmas pageant, because she assigned the parts of Mary and Joseph to Kate and me, and Ott and Elias were given the parts of shepherds. Sam was given the role of an angel.

Kate of course was thrilled to be Mary—that was every little girl's dream at Christmas time. I was excited to be Joseph, with several lines and a two-verse solo to sing. I practiced my lines and memorized them quickly. Learning the song was more work.

The lyrics were pretty easy—as Mary's husband, I was in dismay because my pregnant wife was due to give birth at any moment—but I struggled with some of the notes, so I practiced and practiced until I had confidence that I could hit all the right pitches. I would hum the song to myself as I did my chores each day; and I would even find the song running through my head during school. I felt as though I knew the song forward, backward, and sideways.

Invitations had been sent to everyone in Polk City, and a few posters were scattered around town announcing the event. Finally, the night of the big performance arrived. A light snow began to fall as our wagon pulled into the schoolyard, and the air had the clean scent of winter.

The school, already small to begin with, was crowded. For the pageant, a small stage area had been constructed at the front of the classroom, where Miss Baines' desk usually stood. A platform for the angels and shepherds was on one side, and the dessert table for refreshments afterward was next to the platform.

As we put on our costumes, I hummed the song to myself to keep the notes fresh in my mind.

Finally, everything was in place and the pageant began.

We opened with all the children singing two Christmas hymns.

"Kate, Johnny—you're on," whispered Miss Baines, who was helping as stage manager. Mrs. Hudson began playing the accompaniment to my solo as Kate sat down on the "donkey"—a big pillow with two ears and a tail—and I stepped in front of the stage and began singing.

The first verse went well. I was comfortable and confident—and probably a bit too prideful.

Between verses, I looked around and soaked in the twinkling eyes and warm smiles in the audience. I nodded slightly, acknowledging their recognition, as though they had just finished giving me a standing ovation. I almost felt like saying, "Wait, the best is yet to come," but I humbly refrained.

Mrs. Hudson was nearly finished playing the introduction to the second verse, and I got ready to sing the first note, an F. I hummed the pitch softly to myself, took one step forward, opened my mouth, and suddenly went blank on the first word. I couldn't remember it. I also went blank on the second word and then on the subsequent words as well.

I stood in sheer panic. Mrs. Jacobs, standing off to the side, tried to mouth the words to me as Mrs. Hudson played the introduction to the second verse again. Her mouthing of the words didn't help though; she was rather plump and her cheeks sagged, and I couldn't make out what she was saying at all. Mrs. Hudson finished the introduction and again I failed to start the verse.

Mrs. Jacobs had an anxious look on her face, and that caused me to feel even more of a panic. I stood there, mouth twitching, with no words coming out. Some in the audience started chuckling, and then a few more. I was mortified.

Mrs. Hudson played the remainder of the verse while I stood there, mouth open, feeling like a fool. When the piano finished, Kate and I walked off to the side and into the shadows.

"What happened, Johnny?" whispered Kate.

"I don't know, Kate. I feel terrible."

"Johnny, don't worry, it's okay. You sounded great on the first verse, and maybe people won't know that you were supposed to sing on the second verse."

"I think they know, Kate."

"Johnny, it will be fine. I still think you were the best Joseph there ever was. The real Joseph probably could have taken lessons from you, you seemed so real."

I wouldn't have expected my younger sister to provide such encouraging words, and I felt a bit better after her soothing comments.

The next scene—the angels appearing to the shepherds in the fields—took place with the shepherds on the platform, which for this scene was their field.

Sam stepped up onto the platform to deliver his lines as the lead angel, and both Elias and Ott stepped aside to make room for him. Elias turned to acknowledge the angel, but his staff hit Ott in the chest, sending him tumbling backward off the edge of the platform. Ott landed on the dessert table with a crash, his elbow in the center of Mrs. Ritchey's apple pie, his head buried in Mrs. Egleston's chocolate cake, and his back side flattening Mrs. Hudson's buttery pound cake.

Undaunted, Ott hopped back up on the platform and delivered his lines as pieces of chocolate cake fell off his head and onto the stage, leaving the audience howling.

Afterwards, the reception that Mrs. Jacobs had arranged was quiet. People didn't stay too long, mostly because there were only three plates of cookies that Ott hadn't demolished with his fall. At one point, I saw George standing over in the corner, alone. I approached him.

"Johnny, the first verse sounded good." George smiled.

"George, I really messed it up. The first verse went fine, I think, but I could feel my pride swellin'. Maybe that's why I blew up on verse two."

"Johnny, two things. First of all, forgetting a verse can happen to anyone. And I know it's not like you didn't try—you practiced this thing thoroughly. You gave it your best, so you have nothing to be ashamed of, really.

"The second thing though is this: the pageant isn't about you. It's about the birth of our Savior, Jesus Christ."

"I know that."

"Well Johnny, then don't focus on your mistake—rather, focus on whether anyone in the audience got excited about the message and drew closer to God because of it."

"I ... I don't know, George."

"You weren't paying attention, were you," he said with a smile.

"No, I guess I wasn't. After I went off to the side, I pretty much just sat there, embarrassed."

"Well, I can understand that, but you missed an opportunity to share with a friend. Your buddy Clarence got down on his knees during the prayer time at the end."

"He did? Clarence? Oh, how I wish I could have talked with him!"

"I talked with him, Johnny. I think he's on the right track. Of course, it wouldn't hurt to have the encouragement of a friend like you, who is closer to his age."

"I guess that's my job."

"Right, Johnny. Never forget that God works in mysterious ways. It's not by our own strength or our own cleverness that he accomplishes his work."

That was a lesson I never forgot, and I knew it was true whether things were going well or horribly wrong. I had to also remember the importance of keeping things in proper perspective. I thought my performance in the pageant had been disastrous. It wasn't until we returned home that night that I really saw disaster.

# 36

# Fire

The first thing I noticed on the way home that night was the sky. The clouds had cleared up enough during the program so that the moon, nearly full, shone brightly on the fresh snow. In fact, I could have read a book outside if I wanted.

The second thing I noticed was the smoke. Even from far away, we could smell the smoke. When Pa realized that the smell grew stronger as we drew nearer to home, he began urging Millie and Billy to go faster and faster. The road between our place and the school had a little rise at about the halfway point, and as soon as we came over that rise, we saw it. Off in the distance, across the prairie and about a mile away, we saw fire.

"Giddup!" yelled Pa, encouraging the horses with the little-used switch that he kept beneath his seat. "Giddup!" The horses raced with a speed I had rarely seen, almost as though they could sense the urgency in Pa's voice.

"Pa," said Kate, "Is that our house?"

"Yep," replied Pa, softly but firmly.

"Oh, no!" cried Kate, and she began sobbing.

Elias wrapped an arm around her and she tucked her face into his shoulder.

As we neared home, Pa began shouting out instructions. "George, prime the pump and get water flowing. Everyone else—we have buckets behind the barn. Elias, Ott, Johnny, and Kate, grab the buckets as soon as we get home."

I was on my knees in the corner of the wagon, peering around Ma, as we pulled into the farm yard. Despite the urgency of the situation, my eyes noticed something and I immediately spoke without thinking. "Pa, look at those tracks in the yard. They look like buggy tracks."

Pa didn't say anything—there wasn't time—but I could tell that he looked in the direction of the tracks in the fresh snow.

The flames engulfing the house roared high into the night sky. The fire had not yet reached the barn.

The wagon halted to an abrupt stop just inside the farm yard.

"Go!" shouted Pa, as we all jumped out of the wagon and headed for the barn, except for George, who ran to the pump. As we ran behind the barn to get the buckets, I noticed tracks—footsteps maybe—going off into the orchard. I didn't think anything more of it at the time.

We ran to the pump and began filling buckets.

"The barn," Pa yelled, "throw all the water on the barn!"

"But Pa," Elias exclaimed, "the house! What about the house?"

"The house is gone," said Pa, "but we still have the livestock. Get them out of the barn. Let's go!"

Ott and Elias opened the door and began bringing out the animals. The rest of us began drenching the side of the barn with water.

With a deafening crash, the roof of the house collapsed, and a rush of fire billowed upward.

"The barn roof, John, water the roof!" shouted Ma.

"Make a line. We'll pass water up," yelled Pa.

    The heat emanating from the house was fierce, and sparks were flying through the air, blown by the wind, and landing on the barn. We formed a bucket line and soon water was being poured on the barn roof, but the flames were coming faster than we could put them out.

Just when it seemed we were losing the battle to save the barn, a wagon pulled into the yard and stopped next to ours. It was the Hudsons!

For the next hour, the Hudsons helped us keep the barn sufficiently wet to prevent it from burning, and we poured water on and around the house to contain the fire.

Eventually the fire began to subside. The animals, safely out of the barn, stood by the wagon and showed no inclination to run off into the cold darkness. Exhausted, there was really nothing else we could do other than keep the fire contained and just let it die out.

"John?" said Ma, quietly.

"Yes?"

"We didn't lose everything."

"I know, Catherine. We still have us," replied Pa.

"That's not what I meant," said Ma.

"What then?" asked Pa, looking at her.

"This morning, something prompted me to take our money box and hide it in the root cellar. I wasn't expecting a fire, but it worried me that someone, anyone, might realize we were gone. I also hid the family Bible."

"You put the family Bible in the root cellar?"

"I did. I don't know why, but I did."

Pa wrapped his arms around Ma and hugged her. "I love you, Catherine."

"I love you too, John."

Later, Elias asked, "So whose buggy tracks do you think those are?"

"I have one guess, but I don't want to jump to conclusions," said Ma.

"Me too," agreed Pa. "Old Jack must have put up a ruckus when the buggy arrived."

Old Jack! Where was he?

"Jack!" I began yelling. "Jack!"

Elias and the others looked at me a moment, and then they too realized it—Old Jack was missing!

"The orchard!" I shouted. "There were tracks going into the orchard!" I led the way, and we ran behind the barn and followed the tracks into the orchard. There, on the other side of the apple tree, lay Old Jack. He was motionless.

Elias picked him up and carried him into the barn. "I think … he's still alive," gasped Elias. Ott lit an oil lamp and we all gathered around Old Jack. Sure enough, he was still breathing. His head was bloody, with one eye swollen shut. He didn't even try to stand.

"Let me see him," said Pa, who had followed us into the barn. Pa took one look and grimaced. "If I didn't know better, I'd say he chased somebody out to the orchard, where he was then attacked and beaten."

"Who would do something like that?"

"Somebody who thought Old Jack was in his way … perhaps somebody who found himself face to face with a snarling dog. Johnny, bring me a bucket of warm water."

I ran out to the pump and filled a bucket with water, and I placed it near the burning embers of the front porch. It warmed up quickly, and I carried it into the barn. Pa washed Old Jack's wounds.

"Fortunately he doesn't seem to have been hit with anything sharp. I think he'll be okay." I gave Old Jack a hug.

The Hudsons invited us to stay with them for as long as we needed, an offer that Ma immediately accepted. Pa told Ma to take Ott, Kate, and me to the Hudsons' place and that George, Elias, and he would stay to keep an eye on the barn, the livestock, and Old Jack.

At the Hudsons' house, Ott and I slept in blankets on the floor in front of the fireplace, and Ma and Kate squeezed into beds. It wasn't comfortable, but it was a warm, dry place to stay.

Pa, George, and Elias came over early the next morning.

"Pa?" Kate asked, as we were eating breakfast with the Hudsons.

"Yes Kate?"

"Pa, why did God send the fire?"

"I don't know that he sent it, Kate. But he did allow it to happen, I guess."

"Pa, I know God loves us, but I don't understand why the fire happened."

"Kate, I don't understand everything about this either. I do know that we probably feel closer to God now than we did before the fire. God lets things happen in the world; but he loves us too. Just remember that we are going to be with him forever. We're here on this earth just a short time."

"Pa?"

"Yes Kate?"

"I don't understand most of what you just told me. But I love God."

"That's all you really need to understand, Kate—just love God."

# 37

# From the Ashes

After breakfast, we all went back to our farm. Sheriff Cogswell was there, walking around the charred remains of the house. I could see the smoke still rising in wisps and then disappearing in the morning breeze. The sheriff didn't say anything at first, but he nodded to Pa and Pa nodded back. Pa walked over to get a closer look at the buggy tracks in the snow.

Most of the snow near the house had melted from the heat of the fire, but remnants of the buggy tracks that we had seen could still be found, especially out toward the road.

"John, your thoughts?" asked the sheriff in a soft voice.

"I'm curious about these buggy tracks, Sheriff. They were here when we first returned home from church last night and found the house in flames. It looks like the tracks came in from the road and headed toward the porch."

Pa paused, as if trying to replay the events in his mind, and then he turned and began walking toward the barn. "Sheriff, come with me," said Pa.

"Yes sir," replied the sheriff. I tagged along behind.

"Last night," Pa continued, as we walked past the barn and into the orchard, "we saw two sets of tracks heading out to the orchard—a set of dog tracks and a set of human tracks. I guess the boys and I stepped all over those tracks as we were looking for Old Jack. It looks like there might have been some kind of scuffle over there, under that apple tree," said Pa, pointing. "Sheriff, we found Old Jack lying in the snow just a few yards this side of the apple tree. He had been beaten senseless. Hmm, and there's another set of footprints that I don't remember seeing last night."

"Those are mine," said the Sheriff. "I took the liberty of walking around these tracks just before you got here. How is Old Jack doing?"

Pa glanced at me. "He'll be okay, I think," I said.

"Good, good," replied the sheriff. "Incidentally, John," he said, turning to Pa, "I found this in the snow right where you think a fight may have occurred."

He held up a white handkerchief. The initials HK were embroidered on it.

"Sheriff, are you thinking what I am thinking?"

"I think we need to go into town, John. Can we bring your dog?"

"Sure. Mind if I bring Johnny to keep an eye on him?"

"Not a problem, John."

Elias lifted Old Jack into the wagon and I climbed in and sat next to him.

"You others," said Pa, "should tend to the animals and help your mother sift through the ashes, seeing what you can salvage."

We drove into town, with the sheriff riding his horse alongside the wagon, and stopped in front of the Polk City Bank. "Johnny, stay here," said Pa, as he and Sheriff Cogswell stepped into the bank. Old Jack and I waited in the wagon; and I could tell that he had gotten some of his spirit back. He cheerfully barked at everyone walking by, as though he were inviting folks to come and play with him.

Less than ten minutes later the door opened and out stepped Pa, Sheriff Cogswell, and Mr. Kilpatrick, who was walking with his hands behind his back, hand-cuffed.

They approached the wagon, and Old Jack cowered, backing away from Mr. Kilpatrick with a whimper. "That settles it in my mind," said Sheriff Cogswell. "Come on, Kilpatrick, you're going to be spending some time in jail."

"Nonsense!" shouted Mr. Kilpatrick. "You only have circumstantial evidence. No witnesses, no proof."

"I forgot to mention," said Sheriff Cogswell, "that a member of our community came in early this morning and confessed to stealing Alexander Pierce's bank receipt for you—for a mere ten dollars—so that you could force Pierce into bankruptcy."

"Are you going to take the word of that Slaughter kid over mine?" Mr. Kilpatrick declared.

"And just how did you know I was talking about Clarence?" said Sheriff Cogswell.

Mr. Kilpatrick scowled, refusing to say anything further.

The following day, after the glow of the embers had totally disappeared, we continued sifting through the mound of ashes to see if anything from the house might be salvageable. The stove miraculously was still pretty much intact, even though the roof had fallen on it. The skillets, pots, several handfuls of nails, and a few other odds and ends were also found.

We lost the clothes that we weren't wearing, but we never had that much anyway. All the books were gone, as well as old family letters that Ma and Pa had kept. Pa reminded us that we had each other. After a full day of sifting, sorting, and searching, we cleaned up and headed to the Hudson's house for supper and a good night's sleep.

"This is almost like an adventure, Pa," said Kate.

Ott laughed. "It's not like an adventure, silly, it is one."

Over the next couple of weeks Pa appeared before the judge and jury. When all was said and done, Mr. Kilpatrick was found guilty of several crimes and he had to pay Mr. Shanley and us for all the damage caused by the fire. Mr. Kilpatrick would be in jail for a long, long time.

As for Clarence, he publicly apologized to Mr. Pierce, who forgave him. Sheriff Cogswell told Clarence to keep his nose clean and to stay out of trouble, an order that Clarence promised he would keep.

The day after the Kilpatrick trial was over, we all went to the barn for a picnic dinner. We ate in silence for a few minutes, and then Pa began talking. "Your ma and I have discussed this. With our house gone, this is a good time to try our hand at homesteading."

He let that sink in before he continued. "Moving out to Nebraska, or Kansas, will not be easy. Life is not easy. But I think there's a new life out there waiting for us. Some of you want adventure, and, well, this will be an adventure." He looked at me and smiled.

Where exactly would we go?

As if reading my mind, Pa added, "We are going to homestead somewhere around Arapahoe, Nebraska. Just east of there, we will visit your cousins in Red Cloud, so that we can use their home as a base while we're looking. They sent us a letter last month and told us that there is still some homesteading land available, though we need to go out there soon because the land is being claimed quickly. We hope we can get a quarter section of land near Arapahoe—that is one hundred sixty acres. We'll build a house and we'll get settled in on our own farm, not a farm that we are only renting."

George, Elias, Ott, Kate, and I were silent. What could we say? Pa was suggesting leaving the only home we ever knew.

I think Pa hoped for a more enthusiastic reaction than what he saw in us, so he tried to reassure us. "I know you have close friends here; believe me, you will make good friends out in Nebraska too."

I thought about Sam. I would miss him, but he would be fine. Then I thought about Clarence. How would he do with me gone? He didn't really have other close friends.

"Pa, how soon are we leaving?" asked Elias.

"Elias, I would like to leave by the beginning of February. I realize that's about two weeks from now, but we want to get out there in time for spring planting."

"Pa," asked Ott, "is the dirt in Nebraska as good as in Iowa for growing crops?"

"I don't really know, Ott," Pa replied. "I reckon we'll find out soon enough."

"Well, Pa," said Kate with a smile, "I know one thing. Nebraska dirt can't taste any worse than Iowa dirt." With that, she made a face and then giggled, causing the rest of us to laugh.

The thought of leaving the comfort of a place I knew was unsettling, but after all, where was my home?

My home was with Pa and Ma. My home was with George, Elias, Ott, and Kate. And even beyond that, I knew, deep down, that my home was wherever God would have me lay my head at night.

Nebraska! The new frontier! An adventurous trip lay before us. Maybe we'd see Indians, maybe outlaws. We would be building our own house and starting our own farm. There would be new creeks to explore and new fishing holes to find. I had spent my whole life looking for adventure, and now it was just around the corner.

CPSIA information can be obtained
at www.ICGtesting.com
Printed in the USA
BVHW071138150223
658525BV00001B/24

9 780984 554157